"I have decided," my grandfather said, "that Lori should go for a year to Israel. She can stay with my friend Macovi and his daughter's family. She'll go to school there, travel around the country. An eye-opening experience." He sat back, looking very satisfied. I felt both my parents waving goodbye to me already, relieved they wouldn't have to worry about me—their pot-smoking daughter—while they jogged together in their matching sweat suits.

"I'm not going," I said.

I kept on saying that while we shopped and packed and picked up the airline reservations.

And now I stood in Lydda airport. I had arrived in Israel, but I still wasn't in any big hurry to reach the moshav that would be my home for the next twelve months.

GLORIA GOLDREICH is a graduate of Brandeis University. Her short stories and critical essays have appeared in many national magazines. In addition to writing, she teaches Jewish History at the Jewish Community Center of Harrison, New York.

LAUREL-LEAF BOOKS bring together under a single imprint outstanding works of fiction and nonfiction particularly suitable for young adult readers, both in and out of the classroom. Charles F. Reasoner, Professor of Elementary Education, New York University is consultant to this series.

LORI

Gloria Goldreich

Published by
Dell Publishing Co., Inc.
1 Dag Hammarskjold Plaza
New York, New York 10017

Copyright © 1979 by Gloria Goldreich

Laurel-Leaf Library ® TM 766734,
Dell Publishing Co., Inc.

ISBN: 0-440-94816-9

RL: 7.1

Reprinted by arrangement with
Holt, Rinehart and Winston

Printed in the United States of America

First Laurel-Leaf printing—December 1980

For Jan, Nadya and Eyal Teutsch
of Ramat HaSharon, Israel

CHAPTER ONE

The plane dipped crazily as we zoomed over the Mediterranean, but I knew there was nothing to worry about because the pilot's voice came over the intercom in the same flat, bored tone he had used to tell us that we were flying over Iceland, across the coast of England, high above the Alps. Now he informed us, in his very good English which had just a trace of a Hebrew accent ("charming" my mother would call it), that if we looked out of the windows on the right we could see Famagusta Bay.

Cyprus had been in the news a lot pretty recently, and I had even done a special report on it. Our social studies teacher had divided the class into groups, with each one taking on a different part of the world. The really good social studies students got the common market countries and bored all of us with reports about devaluation and cooperative trade. The two black kids got the Scandinavian countries, and Nils Lundgren, whose father was some kind of consul from Denmark, led the group that took Africa. That was the kind of school Chatham was. Tessie Anatos got Israel and I took Greece and Cyprus. I cut out all these news stories where a group of Greek Cypriots burned the village of a group of Turkish Cypriots or a Turkish zealot cut off the ears of a Greek policeman or a bunch of Greeks slaughtered a goat and poured the blood all over a Turkish mosque. That's why when I looked out the window toward Famagusta Bay I kind of expected to see smoke and dying fires and maybe a couple of pools of blood, but all I saw was this really gorgeous stretch of blue water on which colored sailboats skittered. No fire and blood down there, I decided, and I felt sort of cheated. Not that I wanted anyone to get burned or die, but still, if the papers kept reporting all this gore, I wanted to see some of it. I guess I have kind of a gruesome tendency. That's what my father used to say when I would lean far out of the window when we passed an accident on the highway.

"Lori's bloodthirsty," he'd say. "The child's absolutely gruesome."

I wanted to explain then that I just wanted to see so that I would understand what was happening, but it was hard to explain anything over my mother's giggle and his deep laugh, to say nothing of the music they always had playing on the tape deck as though they were afraid of it ever being quiet enough in the car so that they could really talk to each other. Of course, all that was long ago, before my mother went back to law school and my father went down to Florida to open a branch of the business in Tamarac.

"Isn't the bay gorgeous?" the girl in the seat behind me asked.

Her name was Amy and she thought everything was either gorgeous or terrific. The whole trip she had talked about her gorgeous cousin in Tel Aviv, her terrific friend home in Hartford, and when they gave out those disgusting airplane meals she began talking about how exciting it was to be eating while we were flying. I made believe I was reading when she came back from the john because I didn't want to hear what she had to say about that. She and her friend Ellen were going to Israel for the year on some sort of Zionist course, and they kept practicing the three Hebrew sentences they knew. I couldn't stand listening to Amy and Ellen go over the same sentence again on what a nice day it was in Tel Aviv, was it nice in Haifa too or did it rain fall there? They never could remember the word for rain and were always turning to the back of the book.

"Geshem," I wanted to scream. I'm pretty good at languages—not that it ever would have occurred to me to study Hebrew even if they gave it at the Chatham School, which they don't. But then, I can't say that Israel would have been my choice of a place to spend a year. I was only on that

plane because my grandfather started playing the heavy. Probably I would have chosen some place that wasn't so darn far away. I felt as though I had been on the plane forever listening to those two girls discuss the weather patterns in Tel Aviv, even though I knew it was only ten hours since we had left New York. I yawned, fell asleep, and didn't wake up again until I heard the pilot say in a voice that wasn't bored anymore but really happy and excited—"We are now flying over the coast of the State of Israel. Shalom and welcome!"

The loudspeaker played a record of some Hebrew song and most of the passengers began singing. Amy and Ellen were singing and crying, falling all over each other to look out the window. A group of bearded men had gone to the rear of the plane and were praying. They bent and swayed, wrapped in their white prayer shawls with the leather phylacteries wound around their arms and their foreheads. My seat mate, a little old woman wearing a wig, who had spent the whole trip crocheting skull caps, looked out the window and smiled. It was such a happy, peaceful smile, it made me feel awfully lonely suddenly, and I looked out the window too. But all I saw was a strip of water as blue as Famagusta Bay and a patchwork quilt of green grass and brown fields, toy houses and toy cars. It was pretty, but I couldn't understand why it was making people laugh and cry and pray.

There was more singing and crying at Lydda Airport as we disembarked. Behind the wire gate people were waving frantically and screaming out names.

"Rivkale. Little Rivka. Here, I'm here," a man called and my bewigged neighbor turned around and smiled, her eyes filled with tears.

"It's my brother, Chaim," she said to me. "I haven't seen him for almost twenty years. Look, see how good God is."

I wanted to ask her what was so good about a God who kept a brother and sister apart for twenty years, but I've stopped asking that kind of question. It makes people angry and they never answer anyway.

A group of kids from a kibbutz youth movement had come down to meet Amy and Ellen and the others in their group. They carried a big banner with the word "Shalom Chaverim" printed on it, and every couple of minutes they sang another song. Amy and Ellen kept hugging each other and jumping up and down like kids on their first day of camp. I moved away. I didn't want anyone to think I was connected with them. I knew right away what Kenny and Bert and Marcie and the other kids in my crowd would think of Amy and Ellen. "Straights," they'd say in the dry, lazy tone I used to practice at night with a whole string of their exclamations. "Definitely O.K. A drag. Real greasers. Grinds."

I did all right on the "definitely O.K." and when I'd had half a joint I could even manage a "no way" and sound right.

"Listen, here's the address of our kibbutz. If

you ever come there, please visit us," she said. "Where will you be staying?"

Amy pressed a piece of paper into my hand, and I stuffed it into my pocket. She really wasn't a bad-looking girl, if she'd get rid of that dumb shirt dress with the button-down collar.

"On a moshav in the north—a sort of collective settlement. I'm staying with a friend of my grandfather's. He's supposed to meet me here, but I don't even know how I'll know him. . . ."

I watched them leave, singing some song about going up to the land, and for a second I wished I was going with them. What if my grandfather's friend, this Avraham Macovi, never showed up at the airport? What would I do then? It occurred to me that I could just turn around and fly straight back to New York and call up my grandfather and say, "All right. I tried it your way. The account is clear." The thought made me boil with anger and I began having this mental argument with my grandfather, which I should have had with him back in New York but which somehow never took place, what with my mother crying and my father cursing and me storming back and forth to my bedroom. It was a week of slamming doors and big arguments and wads of Kleenex wherever my mother happened to be sitting for more than five minutes. It was all because of me, but hardly anyone bothered to talk to me except my father who would pull my pony tail and say "So? Are you satisfied? Does all this bedlam make you happy?"

It was as though he thought that I got suspended from school just to send the family spinning. When I told Marcie about it she yawned and said in this sort of professional tone, "Oh, he's just projecting. He likes to be the center of attention. Why else is he always playing the piano in the middle of your parties or putting his name and picture in all those stupid advertisements?" Marcie's father is a psychiatrist and she gets her vocabulary from him, although she says psychiatry is a lot of crap. Once both of us hid in the room just outside his consulting room, and we held a glass up to the wall and listened to his patient. It was a lady who kept talking and crying, and right after she left Dr. Edel came into the room where we were and poured himself a drink and sort of snorted and said, "Thank God that's over," although when he talked to her he'd sounded so understanding and kind.

Anyway all that "bedlam," as my father called it, didn't make me happy, and I was sort of miserable about being suspended. Mainly, I didn't think it was fair. You see, this school I went to—the Chatham School—keeps talking about how it doesn't believe in setting up boundaries and rules. Like they have no dress regulations, and kids can come to class dressed any way they please. Even when Marcie came in painter's pants without a top they didn't suspend her but just called her in to discuss it. They were very big on discussions and what they called a "mature interchange." They didn't even take attendance in class. You had a choice of taking an exam, writing, or just having a discussion with a teacher. I always chose a discussion because I found out my first year that all you had to do was let the teacher talk and give his or her opinion; you agreed or made one or two objections and you got an A. In fact, I've sort of figured out that if you let most adults do that, you get to do what you please and they end up congratulating themselves on understanding you. Anyway, a lot of us had started smoking marijuana joints in the john—just sort of passing one weed around so that each of us got maybe three puffs. That was enough to feel light and dreamy for an hour or so but not enough to really float the way we did after a night of passing around joints at Marcie's house with Bert and Kenny while Marcie played her old Chicago tapes.

Anyway, the school didn't go for our smoking in the john, but they didn't come right out and say "No Smoking." Instead they put up little daisies all over the place and in the flower's heart a cute little message about being considerate of others and leaving the air clean and respecting your mind and body and thinking things through before you lit up. The signs and the flowers were so dumb that they made us laugh.

"Maybe they'll get really creative and put up roses," Marcie said.

"Nah, they ought to draw marijuana blades talking to each other about how damaging they are," Kenny put in.

I mean, how can you take talking flowers seriously? So we kept on lighting up, and then one day Dr. Chalmers walked in and found Marcie and me passing a butt. It happened to be in my hand at the time, so I was the one who got canned.

My mother cried like crazy and my father screamed, and then they both yelled at each other.

"It's because you don't ever bother to supervise her—you're so damn busy with that stupid lawyering of yours. I'm glad you're fulfilling yourself, but what about the child you happened to give birth to in the good old days before women's lib?" my father shouted.

"And what kind of father are you? A bunch of appliance dealers in Boca Raton are more important to you than your own daughter. What kind of a man opens a business a continent away from his family? And hadn't you heard—parenting is a partnership."

My mother stormed away to cry in another room, and I was glad that my grandfather had a big apartment and that they could split to separate battlefields. I didn't agree with either of them, although I wished my mother would stop sounding like a page out of Ms. magazine. Parenting. That's not even a verb. And if I lit a joint it was because it made me feel good, not because she was in court when I got home from school or he was in Florida. Maybe Marcie was right. Neither of them was happy unless they were stage center, even when it was my scene.

Only my grandfather stayed calm, smoking cigarillos and placing overseas phone calls. That's one thing about my grandfather. He never gets upset. He just keeps stroking his thick, white moustache or polishing his tiny, rimless eyeglasses and saying things like, "We'll work it out. Discouraged you shouldn't get. It's always darkest before the dawn." My grandfather was born in Germany, and he learned most of his English from magazines, and it's funny sometimes to hear him use these slang expressions and cliches with a German accent. But this time I didn't feel much like laughing. Marcie told me that the kids at school had been so worked up about my suspension that they were going to organize a protest demonstration or a hunger strike or something, but then they had a speaker from Amnesty International and they got turned on to having a teach-in about the treatment of political prisoners in Latin American countries and sort of dropped my case. I wasn't surprised. That's the way the kids in my school are. Any cause will do.

Finally my grandfather called us all together for a meeting. We sat in his study, a big room that overlooks the park, with a lot of leather furniture that smells of tobacco and a telex machine that never stops ticking. My mother and father sat together on the couch. They had come to some sort of truce because my father's hand was on my mother's shoulder and she left it there. They were wearing matching aqua leisure suits which I guess my father had bought for both of them as a peace offering. They already had matching digital watches, sweat suits, and bathrobes. After any really big fight my father always comes home with two boxes. I guess Marcie is right. My parents are like kids themselves. They looked like kids that day in grandfather's study.

"I decided," my grandfather said, "that Lori should go for a year to Israel and I spoke with my friend Macovi who tells me there's a good school not far from his moshav. Lori could stay with him and his daughter's family—there's a child her age in the house. Go to school there, travel around the country. An eye-opening experience." He sat back, looking very satisfied, and plucked a message from the telex which he crumpled and threw on the floor.

"Why a year?" my father asked.

"Because she's suspended from the Chatham School for a year. And the other schools that will accept her with such a record, I wouldn't send her to. And because in a year you get to learn a language, to understand a country."

"But why Israel?" my mother asked.

My grandfather took off his glasses and polished them very carefully. I saw his eyes then, a glinting blue like my own, and they were very bright, the way mine get sometimes when I feel sad or hurt. I guess they got that way when I heard the kids had dropped me for Latin American prisoners.

"That's a nice question a daughter of mine should ask me. When I was Lori's age, maybe a little bit younger or older, the lunatic Hitler came to speak in my town. Macovi and I both went to hear him. Macovi turned to me and said, 'It's time to say goodbye to the fatherland.' We both said goodbye to Germany and both of us were going to go to Palestine. Macovi loved the soil, but I already knew I liked business, liked watching the numbers dance. I decided to go to America, work a few years, and then take the money to Palestine and open a business there. So I came to America and the numbers danced so fast I never got around to going to Palestine. Then Palestine became Israel and I was still here. Always in the back of my mind I was sorry. I felt I had missed something that should have been part of me. I think maybe Lori has this crazy business with the marijuana and the friends that lay around all day in their underwear because she also misses something that should be part of her."

"It's not underwear," I said. "It's tee shirts. Everyone wears them."

"Maybe it's not such a bad idea," my mother said. "After all, it's an international experience."

"Broadening," my father contributed. I felt them both waving goodbye to me already, relieved that they wouldn't have to worry about me while they jogged together in their matching sweat suits. Besides, they never fought my grandfather on anything really important. It was my grandfather's checks that had paid for my mother's law school and my father's new showroom. Like my grandfather would say, you don't bite the hand that writes the check.

"I'm not going," I said.

"You'll like Macovi," my grandfather assured me. "He was a wonderful chess player. You'll play chess with him, Lori."

"I don't play chess anymore," I said. "I'm not going."

I kept on saying that while we shopped and packed and picked up the airline reservations.

And now I stood in Lydda airport watching this customs inspector go through my things, searching each case carefully.

"What is the purpose of your visit?" he asked.

"To hack around," I answered, and I had to smile when I saw him wrinkle his brow. He was a nice man who had tried hard not to mess my stuff up and he was very proud of his English.

"To study," I said, feeling sort of ashamed of myself.

"Well I hope you learn much and well," he said, flashing me a huge smile.

"Yeah, sure. Shalom," I said and passed through the gate that said "Welcome to Israel."

The waiting room was still full, and people were hugging and kissing and talking to each other a mile a minute. The group that Amy and Ellen were with had gone. I searched the crowd but couldn't pick out anyone who resembled Avraham Macovi. A tall man in khaki shorts and a blue work shirt stared at me for a second, then came up to me.

"Might you be perhaps, Lori Mandell, grand-daughter of Henry Sternheim?"

I nodded.

"I'm Chaim Eron, the son-in-law of Avraham Macovi. Welcome to Israel."

"Thanks," I said, but I didn't say anything about being glad to be there. We stood there for a second, staring at each other. I could feel Chaim Eron's pale eyes taking in my jeans, patched in half a dozen places, and the tee shirt that Marcie had given me for a going away present that said "Oui" in huge letters. He picked up two of my valises and I took the hat box.

"Come," he said. "The truck is parked not far. We have a long ride if we want to reach Moshav Balfouria by supper."

I didn't rush to keep up with his long stride. Somehow I wasn't in any big hurry to reach the moshav that would be my home for the next twelve months.

CHAPTER TWO

The trip from Lydda Airport to Balfouria, about fifty kilometers north of Haifa, took about four hours during which Chaim Eron and I probably broke the world's record for silence. I tried, I really did, but no matter what I asked, I received a one-word answer.

"It's a pretty road," I said as we drove north on the Haifa Road. The air smelled sweetly of sea and citrus blossoms, and the children we passed waved to us.

The psychologist at Chatham had once held what they called a "buzz session" on communications and told us that if we wanted an answer we had to ask a question directly. I tried that technique now with Chaim Eron, proud that I knew something about kibbutzim. (Marcie and I had done a report on utopian societies. We got three "perceptives" and two "sensitives" on it, which was the way teachers at Chatham graded you.)

"Do these fields belong to kibbutzim?" I asked.

"No, not to kibbutzim; to moshavim. Like Balfouria," Chaim replied, which was his longest sentence so far.

"Are moshavim different from kibbutzim?" I asked, thinking I was on a winning streak.

"Yes," he answered, and that was that for the next twenty kilometers until he slowed the pickup truck to stop for three soldiers hitching a ride.

I turned around to stare at them as they got in. I had to admit it; I was pretty curious about Israeli soldiers. I had only been five in 1967, when the Six Day War was fought, but I'd heard a lot about it. And the Yom Kippur War had also been a part of my life. The television was never off in our house, and my grandfather even forgot about his stupid telex—he was so busy looking at maps every time there was a bulletin from Israel. He even called Israel because his friend Avraham Macovi's grandson was fighting on the Golan Heights. It occurred to me for the first time that Avraham Macovi's grandson was Chaim Eron's son. Somehow, I'd been so angry about coming to Israel that I hadn't even bothered to find out about the family I'd be staying with. Well, when I went to camp I didn't get a rundown on my bunkmates either. And Israel and camp meant the same thing to me. It was my family's way of getting rid of me. Anyway, I'd have a whole year to figure out who was related to whom. Right now I was more interested in the soldiers who had settled themselves in and were grinning at me.

Each of them carried an Uzi gun. They wore combat boots and crumpled, olive green uniforms, the shirts open at the neck. One of them was a tall redhead with freckles, and the other two were chocolate-skinned Yemenites with very white teeth and enormous dark eyes.

The redhead looked at the patches on my jeans. He winked at me. "Shalom. Okay."

One of the Yemenite boys fished around in his duffle and took out a guitar. He played "Where Have All the Flowers Gone?" singing the words in Hebrew, and the other two soldiers joined in, leaning on their rifles. I picked up on the last verse and sang in English:

"Where have all the soldiers gone?
Long time passing.
Where have all the soldiers gone?
Long time ago?
Where have all the soldiers gone?
They've gone to graveyards every one.
Oh, when will they ever learn,
Oh, when will they ever learn?"

The three boys harmonized with me. We sounded pretty good, and I was sorry when they told Chaim to stop the truck. I waved goodbye to them and watched them disappear over a curve in the road, lugging their guns and singing peace songs. Israel was a crazy country, I thought and I felt pretty lonely suddenly and I wondered whether my father was home or in Florida and what the kids at school were doing. I wondered also whether anyone was wondering about me, and that made me feel like crying because I was pretty sure no one was.

We stopped for lunch at a little cafe, and Chaim Eron ordered for both of us. A small, bare-foot boy brought us pitta sandwiches stuffed with lamb and vegetables, and bottles of coke. It was funny to see the Coca-Cola script in Hebrew let-ters.

"Good?" Chaim asked. He seemed happy to see me enjoying the food.

I nodded.

"My children love kabob, too."

"How many children do you have?" I asked.

"Rina, just your age. Sixteen. Danni, twenty. He is a paratrooper. And Udi." At the last name his voice drifted off. I looked away. I didn't want to watch anyone else's sadness. My own was all I could handle.

The road climbed after we left Haifa, and the air took on a mountain coolness. I pulled on a bright red sweat shirt that said "I'm the Greatest" and saw Chaim Eron glance at it briefly. Darkness was coming on and the sky turned from blue to a pale violet streaked with red and gold. We passed an Arab dressed in an over-large western suit, a white kaffiyah on his head, astride a donkey.

"*Salaam aleihem,* Chaim Eron," he called.

"*Aleihem salaam*, Abdul Nashif," Chaim answered and drove on.

"A neighbor. A friend," he said to me.

I felt again the kind of bewilderment I'd felt watching the clear, blue waters of Famagusta Bay. I thought of all the newscasts I had seen and the films of the Yom Kippur War that showed battlefields littered with the bodies of Israeli boys killed by Arab soldiers and young Arabs killed by Israelis. Yet here, on this quiet mountain road, an Arab and an Israeli passed each other and exchanged greetings of friendship. I felt confused and wished that I was back in Chatham School where everything was clear. War was bad, peace was good.

Ahead of us a small boy led a flock of goats over a gentle hillock thick with red anemones. A little goat stumbled, and the boy, without breaking pace, scooped the tiny animal up and held it close. I remembered falling once, as I trailed behind my mother and father at the Vineyard. My father picked me up and carried me the rest of the way, and I remembered how his chin had scratched my cheek and the smell of lemons on his skin. Angrily, I shook away the memory.

"What's that?" I asked Chaim, pointing to a snow-capped mountain peak.

"Lebanon," he answered. "We are almost at Balfouria."

I fell asleep then and didn't wake up until the pickup truck lurched to a halt. The air was filled with the smell of lemons, and I thought for a moment that I was lost in a dream until I saw the young citrus trees on which the new fruit dangled, lemons shining like gold in the moonlight.

Chaim Eron was out of the truck, and a woman was running toward him, followed by a girl.

"Chaim, you're so late. I was worried." She spoke perfect, if heavily accented, English.

"Ach, Esther, you worry too much. Those days when we had to worry are behind us. A trip to Tel Aviv isn't a dangerous mission now. I'm late because the plane was late, and then I waited for the child. And we stopped for something to eat. She fell asleep. . . ."

He hugged the girl and I saw that she wore her long, dark hair in a single, thick braid down her back. Dark eyes shone out of glowing, tanned skin. She reminded me of a girl in Chatham I had always liked—Mimi Dodd—who had always taken the jobs of coaching the younger kids instead of taking regular gym and who spent every summer on an Indian reservation. I had never gotten to know Mimi because Marcie and the rest of my crowd thought she was sort of weird. Well, they wouldn't keep me from knowing Rina, I thought wryly, and clambered down, stumbling a little so they would think I really had just woken up.

"Ah," said Chaim. "Our guest. Lori, this is my wife Esther; my daughter, Rina. I am sorry, but my father-in-law, Macovi, the good friend of your grandfather, is at a government meeting in Jerusalem."

"Shalom," I said at the same time that Rina said, "Hello." The two greetings collided, and we smiled at each other.

"I'll help with your things," Rina said, and we each took a bag. The small porch was lit by a large citronella candle, and, in the small circle of light that it formed, I could see a young man in a wheelchair watching us. An army blanket covered his legs.

"Lori," Chaim Eron said, "this is my oldest son, Udi."

"Shalom, Lori," Udi said in a dry voice. His eyes rested on my sweat shirt. "What good news you bring us from America. Are you really the greatest?" Swiftly, he turned his chair and wheeled himself into the house.

"Please," Rina said, clutching my arm in apology. "You must excuse Udi. It is difficult for him. He has been like that since the Yom Kippur War. Five years."

"It's okay," I said, but the warmth I had felt at my welcome evaporated.

CHAPTER THREE

The first couple of weeks at Balfouria passed pretty quickly. I had gotten there at the beginning of what they call the *chofesh hagadol*, the long vacation that begins at the end of spring semester and goes on right through the end of the Jewish New Year and the Day of Atonement. It was great that Rina was on vacation and we had time to get to know each other. Not that we really had to work at it. In chemistry, the teacher used to talk about a scientific mystery—how certain compounds, for no reason, were drawn to each other and worked well together. Rina and I were like that. There were also other compounds that set off hostile reactions, and that was what Udi and I were like. We seemed to bristle when we saw each other and I felt angry at him for being crippled because it gave him an advantage.

I had to hold myself back sometimes, not to be nasty to him. Finally we just kept out of each other's way. I was relieved when he left to do a summer session course at the Hebrew University in Jerusalem.

"Udi is a physicist. He's just finishing his doctorate now," Rina explained. "That is, if he will finish. He was almost through when the war began, and since then he's been so depressed that he works slowly—sometimes does not do anything for weeks at a time. Still, he is very brilliant, and Professor Markevitch has great hopes for him. I am glad he decided to go for this course."

It was my secret belief that it was my presence at Balfouria that drove Udi south to Jerusalem, but I didn't mention that to her. My feelings about her brother were one of the few things I didn't discuss with Rina.

Otherwise we talked about everything. I told her about my mother and father and their life together. I told her about how my mother had decided to go back to law school when I was eight years old.

"See, she got married when she was still in college, and I was born about a year after she graduated. She was pretty unhappy when I was small, kind of always looking for things to fill up the day. I remember she took modern dance classes and then ceramic classes. Stuff like that."

"Like children always looking for a new toy, a new game," Rina said thoughtfully. Her words sounded familiar, and I remembered then that

Marcie had once said something like that. The difference was that Marcie said things to be smart-alecky and Rina really thought about everything she said.

"Sort of," I agreed. "Anyway, when she decided to go to law school we sold the house in Mamaroneck and all of us moved into my grandfather's apartment. It's pretty big and he has a housekeeper and a maid and all, so they didn't have to worry about me while they did their thing. My father likes flying off to places, and he started this chain of appliance stores in Florida. And they're really happier now. They each have their own lives and they seem better together."

Rina told me about her parents, whom I called Esther and Chaim because no one at Balfouria used family names—maybe because everyone at Balfouria thought of themselves as one family.

Esther was a sabra, a native-born Israeli, so called after the prickly pear—a desert fruit with thorns on the outside but sweet and soft on the inside. Esther remembered when Balfouria—now a pleasant little village with white-washed houses, neat gardens, even a small post office and a general store—had been a tent city sunk in swampland thick with mosquitoes. Her younger brother had died of malaria, and a sister had died of dysentery from bad water. She had worked with her father at draining the swamps, and there was a picture of her as a small girl in the Balfouria library, putting a sapling tree into the ground. She had learned her English from the British soldiers during the Mandate and had worked in the British district office while she was a member of the Haganah, the secret Jewish army.

"My mother was an intelligence agent," Rina said proudly. "By working for the British she got information the Haganah needed."

I thought of Esther Macovi peeling a mountain of potatoes or crouching in her kitchen garden, setting marigolds out between the tomato plants, and tried to imagine her as a daring spy, living a double life. When I wrote Marcie about her I only put in the part about being a double agent and I left the kitchen garden out.

"My father came with a group of illegal immigrants—all of them survivors of the death camp Sobibor. They came off the boat and went into the Haganah. He left one war and came to another, but this war was his—he was a fighter, not a victim. He didn't know a word of Hebrew when he met my mother, but he did know English. His father had been a professor of English in Budapest. They courted in English, and that is why they still speak it. Also, so we should know it, I think. Everything they do, they have always done, has been because of us—myself and Udi and Danni. It's hard for me sometimes to think that I am so much the center of their lives. I'm afraid always that I will hurt them, disappoint them." She sighed, and I wondered what it was like to be the center of someone's life. My parents were each the center of their own lives, and my grandfather's telex was the center of his. That left me drifting—

the way I'd drifted sometimes after puffing on a joint, feeling loose and free and not even wanting to feel attached.

During those first couple of weeks I fell into the pattern of Rina's days. At home in America, long vacations—when we weren't at the Vineyard house or off on a trip or something—meant sleeping late, then talking to the kids on the phone, and finally getting together to listen to records or go to the village. Marcie's parents had tried sending her to one of those camps that offered everything—workshops in film making, ceramics, even glassblowing—but she only lasted for a week. I was sent on a wilderness survival trip but I got poison ivy; so I didn't survive too long. But for Rina, vacation meant working in the moshav greenhouses. Balfouria exported cultivated flowers to Europe—tulips and gladioli which they grew in neat rows of greenhouses. I was disappointed when I found out about Balfouria being in business. I liked the idea of a community providing for itself—everyone living off the land. When I said so, Udi, who hadn't left yet for Jerusalem, gave me one of his withering looks and said, "Ah, the blood of idealism flows in the veins of our little American cynic."

"At least I've got blood in my veins," I said and stormed out.

Anyway, I worked in the greenhouses with Rina, just doing what she told me to. I liked working among the orderly rows of flowers. Through the misty glass I could watch the world of the moshav drift by—the children on their way to day camp; women going off to market; the men, in their earth-caked work boots and faded khakis, stopping to chat and smoke a cigarette. Almost everyone on the moshav was involved in agriculture, although some of the men had jobs in the cities or did government work in Jerusalem, the way Rina's grandfather, Avraham Macovi, did. I hadn't met my grandfather's old friend yet, but he was due back from Jerusalem soon. He was sort of an elder statesman, and when Esther spoke to him on the phone and asked him about Golda, I knew she was talking about Golda Meir.

"Golda's legs are bothering her," Esther told Chaim.

"She smokes too much," Chaim said.

And it was the woman who had been prime minister they were talking about! I wrote about it in a joint letter to Marcie and the other kids. I'd had only one letter from Marcie and another from Kenny. Marcie wanted to know what the Israeli soldiers were like, but I couldn't answer her because the only ones I'd met so far were the three hitchhikers and a couple of boys from Balfouria who came home on weekends and peeled off their uniforms and got into work clothes. Kenny wanted to know about scuba diving in Elath, but I couldn't even tell him about that either because I hadn't been as far south as Haifa.

I sometimes thought about them while I worked among the flowers—shifting new shoots from one pot to another or carting a load of full-grown flowers to be packed for shipping. Rafi and Gad, a couple of high school kids who worked along with us had great voices. They'd practice a rock routine as they tied the gladioli in bunches. Rafi told me that what they really wanted to do was finish the army, work in a club in Tel Aviv, and get a recording contract. That was what Kenny talked about too, and I was surprised that I had traveled thousands of miles to listen to the same sort of dreams, the same sort of plans.

Evenings, a group of us would gather in someone's living room and listen to Rafi and Gad. I harmonized with them sometimes, and they taught me a couple of Hebrew songs and I taught them some Tom Paxton and Phil Ochs ballads. Rina did a translation of "The Universal Soldier," and I even got to learn it in Hebrew. Everyone laughed at my pronunciation the first time I sang it, but I worked on it, and the next time they sat pretty quietly and Gad worked out a neat guitar accompaniment.

Having a set rhythm to the days and nights helped a lot those first couple of weeks, and sharing a room with Rina was nice. I'd never shared a room before. I used to think of my room in my grandfather's apartment or the one in Mamaroneck as a cave to which I carried the posters and records and books. At Balfouria I was homesick, but I wasn't lonely.

I had grown so used to the pattern of our days that I was kind of thrown when Rina asked me if I wanted to go with her to visit some friends on a kibbutz near Acre. I really didn't want to go. But I didn't want to share meals with silent Chaim Eron who stuck to the safety of short answers. And then, too, I'd received a letter from my mother who apologized for the fact that my father hadn't written even once since I'd been in Israel. "Daddy plans to call this week," she'd written, which meant that she'd be spending time with him and she'd make him call. Well, let him call, I thought, I won't be here.

When I went upstairs to pack, Rina was trying on a pair of khaki trousers and a blue blouse.

"No good," I said. "Use one of my madras shirts."

Then I undid her braid and coiled her hair around in a bun. She looked terrific, especially when I made her put on some of my coral liquid lip-rouge.

"Do I really look nice?" she asked. Her father came to the door, stared at her for a minute, and then looked hard at me and walked away.

"He thinks I'm corrupting you," I said, but Rina didn't answer. She was busy trying on a silver bracelet.

I put on a pair of jeans and an Indian shirt. I untied my pony tail and brushed my hair loose around my shoulders. The sun had turned it the color of the bright yellow gladioli we'd shipped to Oslo that morning. Even my eyebrows were lighter, making my eyes look bluer.

We stood side by side in the long mirror and

gave each other a hug. We were young and pretty and on our way to a good time.

The kibbutz we were to visit was called Sadot HaEmek—the Fields of the Valley—and we traveled as far as Acre in the moshav truck which was filled with the flowers readied for shipment to Norway. In Acre, we went to a sidewalk cafe on the main street to wait for the pickup truck from the kibbutz. As we sipped from tiny, gold-rimmed cups containing bitter, black coffee, Rina kept looking at her watch and glancing up and down the street. An Arab woman in a long, black dress, balancing a basketful of pittas on her head, passed by.

"He's late," she said. "He said he'd be here at five."

"He's not late. It's not even five yet," I answered. "And who's the 'he?' What happened to the 'friends' we were supposed to visit? It looks like there's only one and he's more than a friend."

Rina blushed.

"His name is Yaakov. I met him when I went with my scout unit to the Negev last year, and we have been writing each other since. Twice we met in Tel Aviv. He's very nice, Lori—you'll like him."

Her voice grew very soft, almost shy.

"But why didn't you tell your father about him?" I asked. I couldn't get my parents to sit still long enough to listen to me discuss a friend, but when Rina told her parents even about her new gladiola cross, they listened as though she had just discovered the theory of relativity.

Rina lowered her head.

"My father, you know, is from Europe. There are things he does not understand about the new Israel," she said.

Just then a truck pulled up in front of the cafe.

"Rina!" a boy's voice called, and she jumped up and ran toward him.

I saw the flash of his smile and watched his arms go around her. Then they came toward me.

"Lori, I want you to meet Yaakov Gamliel," Rina said proudly, and I shook hands with a tall, handsome boy whose skin was as black as that of my classmate at Chatham who had been assigned to study the Scandinavian countries.

CHAPTER FOUR

When I was about seven years old, about a year before my mother had started law school and my father had opened the Florida and Arizona stores, my parents decided to spend the summer at some encounter institute in California. My mother explained it all very carefully to me, the way she always did, only her words seemed to get in the way of my understanding. They were going to California, she said, to get back in touch with each other. When I asked her why they couldn't do that in Mamaroneck, she gave me a funny look and talked about honesty and concentration and privacy, but what she really wanted to tell me was that while they were in California I would go to camp. My grandfather took them to the airport, and we stood together while they walked up to the boarding gate. They were both wearing pale yellow slacks and white shirts with little green turtles on the pockets and carrying tennis rackets.

"America is a wonderful country," my grandfather said. "Here the parents go to camp and the children, also."

"They're not going to camp. They're going to an encounter institute. I'm going to camp."

"All right," my grandfather said agreeably, and he took me to the camp bus. I carried a tennis racket, too, and wore khaki shorts, but I had a green crocodile instead of a turtle on the pocket of my shirt. It's funny how you remember things like that.

Anyway, the kibbutz—Sadot HaEmek—looked a lot like the camp I went to that summer. Everyone lived in small, white houses that looked a lot like our bunks, and there was a big building that was a combination dining hall and recreation hall. Another large building was a laundry, and when we passed it we could smell the harsh carbolic soap they used. It reminded me of the detergent they used at that camp. Every building had a pretty flower bed next to it, and the paths were lined with palm trees that bent whenever a strong wind blew up from the sea. Beyond the buildings, the fields stretched for acres and acres.

That first afternoon Yaakov took us around and gave us the history of every building. We peered into the dining room where a group of men and women were setting up for dinner. The long tables were covered with sheets of blue and white checked linoleum, but a pretty ceramic pot of fresh flowers stood on each table.

"The dining room is only two years old. It was all built with kibbutz labor. We worked on it after we were through in the fields. Everyone contributed something to the building. When we opened it Rabin himself came to give the speech," Yaakov said proudly.

"You mean the prime minister took time out to open a dining hall?" I asked incredulously.

Rina nodded.

"We are a small country, and what each group accomplishes is very important to everyone."

"Yeah," I said. I didn't want to argue with her, but I couldn't see then what was so important about opening a dining room.

Yaakov took us to the children's house and introduced us to his little sisters, Yaffa and Tikva. Their skin, like his, was the color of charcoal, and their dark eyes danced in their little faces. They stared at Rina and giggled and whispered until Yaakov gave each of them a playful pat on the behind.

"They are sabras," he said. "Born here in Israel."

Yaakov had been born in Ethiopia and had come to Israel with his parents when he was about eight years old. They were *falashes*—Abyssinian Jews who practiced their own form of Judaism. Later, Rina told me that the ceramic pots that decorated the dining room were of *falasha* design. Yaakov's mother, a skilled potter, had taught other members of the kibbutz the handicraft, and the kibbutz now exported the beautiful ceramic ware to countries all over the world.

Yaffa and Tikva scurried around their big, cheerful dormitory showing us their own little bureaus and the shelves where they kept their toys and games. Someone had painted a smiling sun across one wall, and on another wall there was a mural showing a parade of children in costumes.

"That's the Purim *Adloyada*—a big costume parade," Rina said. "We'll all go next year—in the spring."

I didn't say anything. The spring seemed awfully far away just then.

Mothers, finished with their day's work, were beginning to come into the children's house. Their voices were calm and unhurried, and they bent low to hear what the children were saying. One woman sorted her daughter's clothing and another bent to search for a lost sandal. One blond woman sat on a rocking chair and slowly braided her little girl's long hair that matched her own. She sang as she worked, and the little girl joined in on the chorus. The woman looked a little like my mother, but her eyes were a sharp green and my mother's eyes are violet blue like mine. Somehow, she made me feel sad. Yaakov and Rina stood in the doorway holding hands, and that made me feel sad too. What was I doing in this country, on this kibbutz? For the first time in a long time I wished I had a joint—something that would lift the heavy feeling that was beginning to weigh me down, a weed to waft me along on soft, floating clouds. It would be nice to share it with someone—to pass the neatly rolled cigarette from one hand to another, feeling the wetness of the other person's lips on the thin paper, knowing that we weren't alone in that never-never land we were gliding toward. I guess that's why we always shared joints—so that we'd have company as we floated.

"Come on, Lori," Rina said. "Yaakov will show us where we're staying."

She put her arm through mine and bent down to kiss Yaffa and Tikva who giggled wildly and danced off to hide in a cupboard. That was one thing about Rina. From the minute I met her at Balfouria I never had to tell her how I felt. She seemed to sense it.

Yaakov had reserved a room for us in a building where young, single people slept, and I was surprised to hear people calling to each other in English.

"We have a lot of volunteers from the States here now, and from England and Australia. They're learning Hebrew and helping with the agricultural work. Very nice people," Yaakov said.

Just then I heard a familiar voice.

"I just love working in the bananas. Isn't it terrific?"

"Fantastic. Exciting."

I turned around and there were my airplane friends, Amy and Ellen. We hugged each other as though we were old friends although all we really had in common was the fact that we were all Americans. Still, that goes a long way when you look out the window and see palm trees instead of pines and the music on the radio is more likely to be an Arabic chant than a rock song.

We talked a little, and they invited us to a party they were giving after dinner that night to welcome a new group from South Africa.

"You go," Rina said when I told her about the party. "Perhaps Yaakov and I will come later."

"You really like him, don't you?" I said.

"Yes. But we do not see each other very often. It is difficult."

"He's never been to Balfouria?"

"No. Please, Lori. Don't ask me to explain what you already understand. My father is a wonderful man, but he is not without prejudice. I have heard him talk about black Jews and even Jews from the tribes of the east—from Yemen and Iraq and North Africa. He does not understand them, does not know them, and it is very easy to distrust and dislike people you don't understand. Sometimes I think there is something within him that must hate as he was once hated."

I thought of Chaim Eron's pale, watchful eyes, his long silences and brief answers, and the way he watched his children—Rina and Udi. I remembered the chain of numbers etched in blue ink into the skin of his forearm. Sometimes his hand reached out to cover the faded numerals, as though he were shielding a wound, covering a blemish.

"When Yaakov and I know each other better—when we know what we really want—then it will be time enough to talk to my father," Rina continued, but I could tell that she was trying to convince herself as much as she was trying to convince me.

"All right," I said agreeably, and my tone sounded uncomfortably like my grandfather's.

I stayed at Sadot HaEmek for about three days and I had to admit that I had a really good time. Although we were there as guests and didn't have to work, both of us put our names down on the work roster. Rina was assigned to the bananas which made her very happy because that was where Yaakov was working that week—and I was asked to help the counselors at the children's house.

"Gee, you're lucky," Ellen said, and I noticed that the level of "fantastics" that generally peppered her speech had dropped significantly. She had been assigned to the laundry two weeks in a row and she kept sniffing her fingers which did smell of carbolic.

"I came here to help build a land, not to do laundry," she said one night, and we all giggled though I could tell she didn't think it was funny.

I could see her point even while I agreed with Amy and Rina's calm arguments that, after all, someone had to do the laundry. Still, I was glad to work with the children, and as soon as Pnina, the head counselor, found out that I could sing and play the guitar, she found me an instrument and I had a terrific time strumming out "Ring-Around-a-Rosy" and "The Farmer in the Dell." The kids played the same circle games and sang the same songs as we had back in Mamaroneck, and after the first day I knew all the words in Hebrew.

I was assigned to little Yaffa's group, and she clung to me wherever we went and I had to admit I liked that. No one had ever waited for me the way Yaffa did; she would jump up in her bed at rest hour when I came in and throw her arms around me, her black eyes sparkling.

"I guess she misses her mother," I told Pnina, a tall girl who wore her dark hair in a shag cut. Pnina had a master's degree in psychology from the Hebrew University, a complete collection of Beatles records, and an army-officer boyfriend.

"I don't think so," Pnina answered. "Our children are pretty happy with the situation. It is the only one they have ever known. Perhaps if they grew up in a conventional home with the mother available all day and then were suddenly faced with our kind of life, there would be a trauma. But Yaffa sees her mother every day. She has grown up here in the nursery. I think she clings to you because she likes you very much."

"Maybe," I said and wandered off to sit by myself for a few minutes and think about what Pnina had said. What I thought about was the years before my mother went back to law school and the maple tree in our yard where my father had hung a tire swing. It seemed to me that one day I had been swaying gently, looking up through the lacy pattern of the leaves, and the next day I was standing by myself in the elevator of my grandfather's apartment house. I was the one who had been jerked from one sort of life to another and I was the one who missed my mother. I was glad that Yaffa found me just then and hurled her little body at me, finally settling herself on my lap while we both looked up to watch the sun slice evenly through the fronds of the palm tree under which we sat.

Evenings at the kibbutz were fun also. One night there was a movie, and everyone pulled chairs out onto the lawn where a screen had been set up and we watched Elizabeth Taylor and Montgomery Clift in *A Place in the Sun*. It was funny to see the subtitles in Hebrew, French, and Arabic, and when the speech was especially long, the words covered the screen. Another evening we had what they called a *kumsitz*, which is really just what the word sounds like. Everyone comes to someone's room and just sits around, talking, singing, playing records, and passing around baskets of nuts and fruits. During the *kumsitz*, people talked about why they had come to Israel. Ronnie, a tall South African engineer, was planning to stay in the country.

"Living in South Africa now is like living in the eye of a hurricane. The situation is dangerous—

very dangerous. But my parents refuse to recognize it and leave," Ronnie said.

"You mean they don't want to come to a safe and quiet country like Israel?" Yaakov asked wryly. Only that morning three Arab terrorists had been arrested a few miles from the kibbutz, and the night watch had been doubled.

"That's not a new situation," Rina contributed. "My father told us that in Hungary the signs of danger were very clear for months before Hitler invaded, but the Jews there did not want to give up their comfortable lives. My father's mother kept on talking about her Meissen tea service and her new living room sofa. My father remembers that she was polishing the furniture the morning the Gestapo knocked at the door."

We were all quiet then and tried to avoid looking at Liesel—a German Christian girl who was spending the year at Sadot HaEmek. Liesel was a pretty, blond girl who belonged to a group of German university students who had volunteered to work in Israel as personal compensation for Germany's crimes against the Jewish people. But Liesel, who had listened quietly, began singing then, her soft, sweet voice rising in the first stanza of "What Have They Done to the Rain?" I picked it up on the guitar, and Yaakov joined in on the recorder. Soon everyone was singing, the lyrics pouring forth in Hebrew, English, German, and French.

I would have stayed at Sadot HaEmek longer, but Rina had a letter from her mother. Esther hoped we were enjoying ourselves and wanted to tell me that my father had tried twice to reach me by phone. Also, Avraham Macovi had arrived home from Jerusalem and wanted very much to meet me.

"It sounds as though we are being summoned back," Rina said. She looked disappointed, and I knew she had wanted to stay on at the kibbutz at least through the weekend because Yaakov was leaving to begin his army service the next week.

"No. I think only I am being summoned back," I replied honestly. "I'll go alone, Rina. I don't mind."

She looked at me doubtfully, but the truth was I didn't mind. I was looking forward to the adventure of traveling alone to Balfouria, of being by myself on the northern highway looking up toward the violet peaks of the mountains of Lebanon. And I was anxious to meet Avraham Macovi, my grandfather's friend.

I kissed Yaffa goodbye and did not wipe my cheek where she had pressed her lips, still sticky from her morning juice. Yaakov and Rina drove me to the Acre Road, and in the jeep I tied back my hair with the purple batik kerchief Pnina had given me when she said goodbye and told me I was always welcome at Sadot HaEmek. I had no trouble getting lifts north. Another kibbutz truck picked me up and I traveled with them until they turned off; then a car of American tourists stopped and took me almost to the turn-off to Balfouria. I had a good time with them in a weird sort of way, pretending I didn't understand English.

"*Ani sabre*," I kept saying with this idiotic grin. "I'm an Israeli."

Then I would sit back and listen to them tell each other how pretty I was and wasn't it amazing that there were so many blond Israelis. And they complained about the heat, their hotels, and their children who never wrote to them. The problem with their children, the women said looking pointedly at me, was that they had too many advantages. If they hadn't had so many advantages they would be sweet and wholesome and innocent like me. I smiled encouragingly. It wasn't often that anyone called me sweet and innocent. When they dropped me off on the Balfouria Road the woman gave me a new lipstick from about fifty that she had in her purse and a package of Life Savers, and I contorted my face into an expression of "wholesome delight and gratitude" and shouted an enthusiastic "shalom!"

I was still giggling when an army jeep slowed and the driver, a good-looking officer, motioned for me to get in.

He asked me something in Hebrew, and when I did not answer, switched to English.

"Where are you headed for?"

"Balfouria. Is it on your way?"

"Yes. Are you staying there?"

I guess because I hadn't spoken to anyone since leaving the kibbutz—a real feat for me—I just needed that question to start me bubbling forth with the story of my experiences in Israel. Or maybe it was the way he asked—the easy, encouraging, interested tone. In any case I told him about getting kicked out of Chatham and how my grandfather wanted me to spend the year in Israel and the arrangements he had made for me to stay wih his old friend Avraham Macovi and the Eron family. I told him how I really hadn't wanted to come to Israel at all and how I'd kept insisting up to the last minute that I wasn't going.

"But now that you are here, what do you think?" he asked.

There was something familiar in his voice, and I looked at him and decided that he had definitely reminded me of Paul Newman. His deep blue eyes crinkled at the corners as though he were used to laughing a lot, and his hair was sort of earth color—thick curls of brown wrestling with gold. I would write to Marcie that night, I decided, and tell her that all Israeli soldiers looked like Paul Newman. That would fix her.

"Well?" he said, but there was no impatience in his tone. He was just waiting for my answer.

"I guess I like it pretty well. I really like Rina Eron. We understand each other. I'm just sorry that she seems to be working herself into a crumb-my situation."

"What sort of situation?"

My mother always told me that she had the best conversations with strangers she met on planes and trains. "You can tell them absolutely anything because you know you'll never see them again," she had said.

That was probably why I felt so comfortable talking to that young officer. We didn't even know each other's name. So I told him about Rina and Yaakov and how she hadn't even told her parents he existed.

"I think Yaakov is a terrific guy, but Rina's father is sort of prejudiced. And he's not the easiest person to talk to—even though he's not as bad as her brother Udi. I know he was badly wounded and all that and I should be more sympathetic—but Udi is the most negative person I ever met."

"Perhaps you're judging him too quickly," the officer said.

"Nope. He judged me too quickly. I just hope the grandfather—Avraham Macovi—likes me. I don't even want to meet the son who's in the army."

The jeep slowed down as we came to a stretch of unpaved road. Two Arab children playing in our path scurried out of the way and ran toward their mother, a slender woman in a long, purple dress who was pruning an olive tree. I looked at the trees in the silvery grove, gnarled and twisted with time, their graceful branches heavy with the hard, green fruit. The bark of the trees was coarse and gray, but I knew that the wood of the tree was a beautiful brown that curled and curved into gentle patterns and could be shined to a satin sheen. Like everything else in this small, complicated country, its surface deceived, and its beauty had to be taken carefully from beneath layers of protection.

"Salaam," the woman called to us.

"Salaam, Hulda Nashif," he replied.

I remembered the name and realized that the woman must be related to the Arab on the donkey whom I had seen when I first came to Balfouria with Chaim Eron.

"Do you live near here?" I asked, feeling suddenly uneasy.

"Yes," he said and swerved into Balfouria, winding through the narrow streets of the moshav with practiced ease until we pulled up in front of the Eron house. Esther was in the garden, plucking newly ripe citrons from the tree, and she dropped her basket and hurried toward us.

"Danni!" she exclaimed and hugged him, smoothing back his tangled curls as though he were a small boy who had just come in from playing. "How fortunate that you were able to give Lori a lift."

"Yes, wasn't it?" he said and smiled, his blue eyes flashing across my face.

But I turned away and shouldered my knapsack, pasting a polite smile on my face.

"Thanks," I said, walking past him and up to the porch where an old man, his head crowned with an aureole of cotton-white hair, stood watching me.

"Shalom, Mr. Macovi," I said, "I'm Lori Mandell. I want to thank you for inviting me here."

I wondered why my face felt so hot and why my eyes burned and I realized suddenly that I felt like crying. I never cried. I didn't even cry when I was kicked out of Chatham. This crazy country was screwing me up.

"Shalom, Lori," the old man said, and he took my hand and pressed it between his own two large hands. His skin was rough and dry and his blue eyes—the same color as Danni's—sparkled with warmth and welcome. "We're very happy to have you here."

"Thanks," I said and went into the house, managing to pass Danni without looking at him.

CHAPTER FIVE

I was up early the next morning and I moved quietly through the kitchen, getting my own breakfast. The air was hazy with the first light of dawn, and the wind chimes which Rina had hung at the window jangled as a strong wind blew down from the Lebanese mountains. I shivered even though I wore a heavy, blue sweater over my jeans and I was glad when the kettle whistled softly and I could make my cup of Elite instant coffee.

"Do you have enough water in there for me?"

My grandfather's friend, Avraham Macovi, stood behind me. In one hand he held a walking stick carved from an olive wood branch and in the other, a basket of brown eggs with scraps of straw clinging to the fragile shells.

"Sure," I said and mixed a cup for him while he

"I like Israel," I said cautiously, following another Chatham rule—any answer will do. Communication, not content, was what adults wanted.

"But Balfouria you're not so sure about?" The old man was a lot shrewder than my guidance counselor, I decided.

"I like Rina a lot," I said. "And I love working with the flowers."

"And Udi and Danni?"

"Udi and I don't like each other at all. I just met Danni and I guess I talked too much to him."

"That he did not say. He only said that you were friendly and laughed a lot. But he didn't seem to think you too talkative." Avraham Macovi threw me a puzzled look, and I realized that Danni was not going to pass anything I had said on to his family. Relief flooded over me with the same speed as the mountain sunlight. I arched upward to the new golden warmth and squirmed out of my sweater.

"You must be a little patient with my family," the old man continued. "This is a strange time for them. Chaim, my son-in-law, has had a very hard life—first the concentration camps in Europe; his parents died, two brothers, and a sister. Rina and Danni are named for the brother and sister and Udi they called for the biblical quote which speaks of an *ud*—a lamb, saved from the flames of destruction. They called their firstborn Udi and yet he was almost consumed by those flames. This bewilders them. They are used to being in control—Chaim and Esther. In the War for Independence they controlled their own history and their nation's. They worked at building Balfouria, controlling and subduing natural forces—the swamp, the climate—and they won. But now their children are growing, and they cannot control their lives. And you, too, puzzle them—as you must puzzle your grandfather. Tell me about my old friend."

"I'm not so hard to understand," I protested but I really didn't want to talk any more about myself and so I talked about my grandfather. I told Avraham Macovi about the apartment high above Central Park West and the whirring telex machine and the ringing telephones with my grandfather barking "sell" into one receiver and "buy" into another.

"Ah yes. When we were boys and went once on a trip to Paris, your grandfather wanted to stay all day in the Bourse."

"And you?" I asked.

"I? I wanted to go southward to the vineyard country, to the farmlands. But if my old friend had not such great success with the numbers in America, here at Balfouria we would not have a library or a recreation hall."

"What do you mean?"

"I mean that it is your grandfather who paid for our library and our recreation hall. You did not know that?" he asked.

"No," I replied and I wondered if my parents knew and was sure that they did not. If they had known they would not have been so surprised when my grandfather decided to send me to Israel. But I didn't have much time to think about it just then because we had pulled off the main road and the truck lurched along across a narrow, rutted path. The only way I could stay in my seat was to grab at its edge. Avraham Macovi bounced up and down, his face red with concentration, clearly enjoying himself, although he leaned back in relief when he pulled into place at last in front of a small, stone house set in a grove of olive trees.

"We are arrived," Avraham said. "Yala Abdul Nashif!"

He climbed down from the truck and I followed him. The door of the house opened, and the Arab man I had seen that first day came out wearing that same over-sized, dark, American suit. His kaffiyah was of a wonderful gauzy material, and I thought it would make a great shirt. Maybe Avraham could tell me where I could buy it and I could get a couple of yards—maybe even make a shirt to send back to Marcie. There had been a record from her waiting for me when I got to Balfouria yesterday—a Wings album—and a note from Marcie telling me that a whole gang from Chatham had gone to a concert together and turned on afterward. It was funny but I didn't even feel bad about missing the concert. It was great of Marcie to send the record, though, and I would definitely make her a shirt.

Abdul Nashif shook his head suddenly, and I saw how his kaffiyah whipped around in the wind. He dug his hands into his pockets and bent close to Avraham who had to stand on tiptoe to talk to him. Avraham wore khaki shorts and a blue work shirt opened at the neck, but both men looked absolutely at home in the olive orchard in spite of the difference in their outfits. Each in his separate way fit into the landscape the way the fishermen at the wharves along the Cape fit into their world. The two men were speaking in Arabic which meant I didn't have to listen, and I was happy just to look around. In the back of the house a couple of scrawny chickens were scrambling for the grain that a small, barefoot boy tossed to them from a metal plate. Near him, an older girl bent over a washtub, beating a pale blue garment against the soapy water. She must have felt me looking at her because she turned suddenly and flashed me a shy smile.

"Hello," I said. "I mean, shalom. I mean, salaam."

"Hello is all right." She stood up and walked toward me, wiping her hands against her simple purple dress. "I know English a small bit. I study at the convent school. I am Nimra—the daughter of Abdul Nashif."

"And I'm Lori Mandell. I'm staying with Mr. Macovi."

"From America?"

"Yes. From America."

She looked at me very carefully, studying my clothes and my shoes, my turquoise and silver necklace.

"I study about America," she said. "Maybe one

day I will study in America. Your friend, Mr. Ma-covi, is a good friend to us."

"To me too," I said and I realized that Avra-ham Macovi had a talent for friendship and people the way some people have a talent for music or for art.

"Nimra!" Abdul Nashif motioned to his daughter who hurried inside. Minutes later she and her mother emerged carrying a large, copper tray which they set down on a small rock on which it balanced easily. They carried out three small leather stools, and Avraham sat on one and motioned me on to another. Abdul Nashif took the third. The two women carried out tiny, carved cups and a copper *finjan*, a double-tiered, slender pot for brewing coffee over open fire. They poured out the thick, black liquid in our cups and came out again with a plate of small, sweet poppy-seed cakes. We sat in the shade of the olive tree, and I rolled the thick, bittersweet coffee about on my tongue and, at Abdul Nashif's insistence, bit into a poppy seed cake. He watched anxiously as I ate it, and when I had finished it and shook my head to indicate that it was good, he smiled happily, revealing three gleaming gold teeth in front, and pressed another cookie on me.

As I bit into it I heard the purr of a Vespa's motor and looked up to see Danni striding toward us. He was not wearing his uniform and seemed younger somehow in dungarees and an open-necked plaid shirt.

"Danni, shalom," Nimra called and darted inside to fill the plate of cookies. She brought one to him, holding the tray out shyly, her skin almost the color of the shimmering copper.

"Shalom, Nimra," he said and took a cake. Their eyes met and it seemed to me that they flashed questions and reassurances at each other, but they said nothing until Avraham and Abdul walked off to one of the small outbuildings. Then they walked together and stood beneath a grape arbor, their heads bent close, talking urgently to each other. I poured myself another cup of coffee and tried not to watch them and wondered why I should feel a strange pang as Danni's thick earth-colored curls bent close to Nimra's glossy, black hair, pulled back into a loose bun. They were old friends and had surely played together as chil-dren; shared those sweet carefree years before he put on his country's uniform and she went off to the convent school. When the two men came toward them again, Nimra went hastily into the house and Danni busied himself examining a vine, plucking a plump white grape that glowed softly in the bright sunlight. He brought it over to me.

"Taste it," he said. "A champagne grape. But one day we will develop one at Balfouria that will be even sweeter. That is what I will work on when I am at the Agriculture Faculty at Rehovoth after my army service. Unless Nimra beats me to it."

"Nimra?" I asked, surprised.

"Yes. That is what we were talking about. She will begin studying at Rehovoth this year. One of the first Arab girls enrolled in the Hebrew University Faculty of Agriculture. Her family is still opposed, but my grandfather has arranged for a scholarship and found her an Arab family to board with. She is certain that in the end her father will allow her to go."

"Gee, I hope so," I said and felt a sweet relief. I noticed for the first time how large Danni's hand was; yet his fingers were slender and graceful.

That grape was not the only gift I received that morning. Avraham Macovi came to me carrying a tiny camel whose left foreleg was bound up in a splint. The animal's large, liquid eyes looked up at us in a mute, dark plea.

"Lori, this creature, only four months, fell and broke his leg. Abdul mended it as well as he could, but he cannot keep him. The other animals will harm him, and he will never be as strong and useful as they will. If we do not take him, he must be killed. Would you perhaps take him into your care at Balfouria?"

I took the small animal into my arms. His body quivered, and I felt his small heart patter wildly just beneath my hand. His fur was as smooth as silk against my cheek, and my fingers felt the delicate bones of his legs and ribs.

"Oh, could I?" I asked, and the three men smiled at each other.

Nimra came up and gave me a halter woven of red ribbons and embroidered with spangles and bells which I slipped around the young camel's slender neck. His very long eyelashes blinked wildly, and then his eyes searched my own and he was quiet.

"He likes you, Lori," Danni said. "What will you call him?"

I didn't have to think for even a moment.

"Why, Shalom, of course," I said.

Nimra's mother looked puzzled and the girl said to her softly, "Shalom—salaam."

"That's even better," I called. "His name is now officially Shalom-Salaam." And I pressed my face against his and giggled when his eyelashes brushed against my mouth.

Shalom-Salaam and I rode back to Balfouria with Avraham Macovi and Danni, who had piled his Vespa on the back of the pickup truck. I loved the feeling of the small animal's quivering body pressed against my own, as though for protection—after all, when had I, Lori Mandell, ever protected anything—and I listened carefully as Danni told me what he knew of the care and raising of camels.

"You see how long the lashes are. That is to keep the sand from his eyes when he goes through the desert. And his fur is short and fine so that the heat will not overwhelm him. You know they call the camel the 'galleon of the desert' because that is how he seems—a tall ship gliding across an ocean of sand."

"Not Shalom-Salaam. I'm going to keep him here with me up in the mountains. I'm going to keep him always," I said, and at that moment the truck lurched over a bump in the road and I felt the tiny camel's heart pump furiously against my own.

"Well, you will have to make plans for him when you leave Israel. I don't think New York City is a good place to raise camels," Danni said.

I laughed, thinking of the attention I'd attract if I walked Shalom-Salaam through Central Park. Probably they'd organize a campaign to get people to scoop up after camels, all because of me. I was still giggling softly when we pulled up in front of the house and Danni pressed my hand.

"Your nose wrinkles when you laugh," he said.

I didn't answer. I had suddenly remembered our ride yesterday and how he had let me babble on and on, betraying my own feelings and Rina's confidences.

"Listen," he said. "I will not say a word about anything you told me. I should have told you sooner who I was, but the truth is, Lori, you didn't give me much of a chance."

"I know," I admitted ruefully.

"Chaverim? Friends?" he asked, and I nodded and handed Shalom-Salaam to him and then climbed down myself.

Esther was furiously mopping down the porch which was piled high with all the furniture from the small sitting room.

"Ah, Danni, I am glad you are back. You can help me to shift the piano. And Lori, please do not leave the house. A call from New York is booked for you and should come through any minute now. What's that you have? A camel?"

She wiped her hands on her apron and took Shalom-Salaam out of my arms, passing her hands gently across his body.

"He is a small beauty. How did he break his leg, Abba?"

"Abdul Nashif thinks that the mother moved too quickly against him, to protect him from young goats who were sniffing about. She tried to do her best for him, poor dumb animal, but in the end she only hurt him," Avraham Macovi answered. "*Nu?* What can you do? Parents sometimes hurt children."

The phone rang then, the staccato, double ring that always seemed to startle everyone at Balfouria, as though the phone were a strange object, foreign to the pattern of their lives.

I followed Avraham Macovi inside and listened to him bark a "shalom" into the receiver which he then handed to me. There was a series of clicks, and then my father's voice boomed on.

"Lori, baby, how are you? We're in Florida. Your mom's here, too. She finished a case, and we're going to take a walking trip through the Everglades. We've got these zippy new backpacks."

"Matching?" I asked.

"Yeah. Bright orange. How did you know? Listen, babe, how do you like it over there?"

"It's all right," I said. Avraham Macovi was peeling an orange, and I watched him twirl the rind off and swing it in a single piece from the end of his knife.

"Well, we had a call from the Chatham School,

and they say it's all right for you to come back this fall. What do you think?"

"I've got a camel," I said. "I have to take care of this camel."

"You mean you want to stay?"

"And I haven't seen the country at all. And I'm beginning to learn a little Hebrew. I'd just as soon stay." I didn't want to sound too enthusiastic or positive because then my father might think I was sick or something; so I kept it low-keyed.

"I'll put your mother on. Whatever you want honey. We love you."

"Sure," I said and felt my eyes getting hot. It was probably true. They did love me. I just got in the way of their walking trips and law cases and showroom openings.

"Lori—you're sure you want to stay in Israel?" My mother's voice was calm, questioning. She'd picked that up in the Parent Effectiveness Training sessions she took at the Chatham School last year when she was between cases.

"Yeah," I said.

"It's your decision," she said. "We only want what's best for you. And this is an enriching experience."

"Right. You okay, Mom?"

"Fine. Take care, Lori."

"You too."

I waited for her to hang up first, the way I always did, even though that soft little click, traveling over ten thousand miles, made me feel kind of sad, as though something had ended. Then I hung up myself.

In the front room there was the sound of furniture being moved and Esther's annoyed voice saying, "We must hurry, Danni. It is just a few days until the holidays."

From the greenhouse across the way I heard Rafi and Gad singing a new song that they had written. My Hebrew wasn't good enough to make out most of the words, but I could tell that it was about seasons passing; the refrain, which they sang in harmony was, "Goodbye beloved, farewell, beloved." Avraham Macovi had peeled an extra orange for me, and I sat down opposite him. The juice dribbled down my chin, and he handed me a napkin that I used to wipe it away and to dab at the tears that were suddenly streaking across my cheeks; tears that I didn't understand. After all, what did I have to be sad about?

CHAPTER SIX

Rosh HaShana, the Jewish New Year, fell on the anniversary of my second month at Balfouria. It was Rina, who had a big thing for birthdays and anniversaries, who thought of that and baked me a cake with two Jewish stars on it. We had it with coffee after our lunch on the afternoon of the new year.

"What will you do when she's been here for a year?" Udi asked unpleasantly, as he ate a slice. "Twelve stars are going to make that cake awfully crowded."

"Maybe we'll have twelve cakes with one star on each," I said.

"Ah yes. The American way. Nothing is too much."

"Better than some Israelis for whom anything at all is too much. Even politeness."

I hadn't meant to quarrel with Udi who had only arrived home from his course in Jerusalem the week before. I had made all sorts of resolutions about being amiable and paying no attention to his sarcasm and I really felt good walking back from synagogue that afternoon.

The synagogue at Balfouria was a little white house which, Rina told me, was the first public building the community had built. Fresh flowers, carried over from the greenhouses that morning, stood in front of the ark which was carved of olive wood and contained the torah. The torah itself was very old and draped in green velvet vestments wonderfully embroidered in gold. Rafi's grandfather had brought it with him when he arrived at Balfouria from Czechoslovakia after the war. All during the war it had been hidden in a forest, and although all the Jews of the town had died in concentration camps, except for Rafi's grandfather, the torah had survived and had a new life in this Jewish mountain village in the Galilee. Danni, who had to go back to his camp right after lunch, wore his uniform when he led the prayer: "May He Who makes peace in the universe make peace over Israel"; and I thought that that was sort of sad and beautiful—to have someone wearing the uniform of war sing so sweetly of peace. I remembered the soldiers who, on my very first day in Israel, had sung "Where Have All the Flowers Gone?"

I was feeling soft and mellow after the service and I was mad at myself for letting Udi drag me into an argument. After lunch I finished helping Rina with the dishes and went off to the small barn where I kept Shalom-Salaam. He limped over to say hello, and his big tongue danced around, limbering up for the treat I always brought him. This time it was a piece of apple dipped in honey. We had eaten them with our lunch, and Chaim Eron had explained to me that apples dipped in honey were always eaten at Rosh HaShana as a sort of edible prayer for a year of sweetness and plenty. I didn't think Shalom-Salaam should be left out.

"See, he likes it. He is a Jewish camel."

Danni had come in so quietly that I hadn't heard him move toward me across the straw-colored floor.

"But he likes goats' eyes, too, so he must be an Arab camel," I said.

"Perhaps he is a universalist. And he is getting to be a strong universalist, too. You take good care of him. When I come next time I will remove the splint." Danni bent to examine Shalom-Salaam's delicate leg, his long fingers probing the bone but releasing it as soon as the small animal whimpered.

"When will that be?" I asked, trying to keep my voice light.

"In two months' time I will get leave. Or at least at Chanukah. But I will be back soon for Yom Kippur. And you will be busy. You start school this week, don't you?"

"Yes. Chanukah—that's almost four months

away?" This time I couldn't keep my voice light. Marcie would have been ashamed of me because I was breaking one of the first rules of the Chatham girls' bathroom—Never Let Him Know How You Really Feel—but I couldn't help it.

"We will plan a trip then. I will try to get a jeep. Perhaps to Jerusalem. And please, Lori. Try not to mind what Udi says. He has been hurt and now he tries to hurt others."

"But why me?" I asked and I didn't like the plaintive note in my voice. It reminded me of a kid I'd known in grade school in Mamaroneck who always said "Why me?" whenever we asked him to do anything.

"Because you are young and strong and beautiful. And free of war and danger."

"Beautiful?" I couldn't keep the disbelief out of my voice.

But he didn't answer. Instead he put his arms around me and kissed me hard, his lips pressing against mine, and then his hands moved upward, passed through my hair and loosed it from the ribbon I wore around it.

"Beautiful," he said and moved toward the door. We looked at each other for a moment, across the soft shadows that flickered over the straw-covered floor, and then he shoved the door open and hurried out. The barn was flooded with sunlight and Shalom-Salaam moaned softly.

I stood still for a minute and then lifted my arms to tie my hair back, but instead I ran my fingers through it and let it lie loosely across my shoulders. I heard Danni's jeep pull away, and when I came out of the barn Udi looked quickly down at the scientific journal he was reading. I knew then that he had been watching the barn, and I wished that I had tied my hair back after all; but, strangely, I was glad that I hadn't.

Danni did not come home for Yom Kippur. There was an alert for infiltrators after a terrorist attack in a northern village, and a lot of soldiers were assigned to patrol.

"It's ridiculous," Udi said. "The Arabs won't attack on Yom Kippur again."

"Yes. It would be good to think that on holy days we could be free of war. But you know, in Europe most pogroms occurred around Christmas and Easter—the festivals of peace and life," Avraham Macovi said.

"This is not Europe. This is a new world, a new life," Udi retorted.

I looked up. For Udi Eron, such statements constituted positive thinking.

"There is no new world, Udi. People remain the same." Chaim Eron had been reading the paper, the lines on his forehead growing deeper and deeper. "Look, I have just finished reading an article on the port strike in Haifa. Everything is self-interest. Do these people think of the country? They think only of their own salaries. They have the mentality of the *mellah*!"

"Is the mentality of the *mellah* so different from the mentality of the ghetto?" Avraham Macovi asked his son-in-law. I wasn't sure exactly what they were arguing about, but I knew that the *mellah* was the Jewish section in Arab and African countries just as the ghetto had been in European countries.

"Very different. *We* came here to build a country. *They* came here to benefit from our labor. Do you remember when we worked on the port? Would anyone have thought of striking then?" Chaim asked.

"True. These are different times. But is it wrong for workers to demand their rights? To want better lives for their families?"

"Did they have better lives in Morocco and in Ethiopia? No. But here they want only to strike—not to work."

"Abba!" Rina's voice, usually so gentle, was harsh with anger now. "The Jews from Ethiopia and North Africa are hard workers, good people. It's not fair to talk about them like that."

"Rina, listen to your father. I know the world and you don't."

"I know more than you think," Rina said and ran from the room.

"Rina!" Her mother started after her, but Chaim put his arm out.

"Let her go. She'll learn."

I didn't say anything but I felt Avraham Macovi's blue eyes, the same color as Danni's, staring hard at me. There was little that escaped the old man's notice, and I thought that he must know that I shared Rina's secret.

My friend had returned from her visit to the kibbutz wearing Yaakov Gamliel's small, black ring on a gold chain around her neck. She had shown it to me the night she returned, and I had touched it, startled by the warm feel of the black stone and the finely etched inscription.

"That is Amharic work," Rina had explained proudly. "His father's carving."

"It's beautiful," I had said honestly, marveling at how the ancient calligraphy, practiced in secret, had emerged from the shadows of centuries and flourished now in Israel.

Rina slipped the ring back beneath her blouse.

"You know what this means?"

"Yes. But you should tell your family."

"Not yet."

Rina had been right.

I followed her upstairs a few minutes after she ran out of the room and found her sitting at the window, looking out toward the mountains of Lebanon.

"You see," she said. "You see why I can't tell them." Her fingers caressed the small, black ring and she held one of Yaakov's letters.

"I see," I said and I sat with her as the purple shadows of evening moved across the sloping mountainsides.

Pnina came from the kibbutz to spend Yom Kippur with us. Rina and I had both become friendly with her at Sadot HaEmek, and though she was a few years older than we were it didn't seem to matter. Pnina was writing a paper on different approaches to child-rearing on kibbutz and on moshav, and Rina had invited her to visit Balfouria and observe the children there. She had taken us up on the invitation, and we met her bus on the main highway just about an hour before sundown.

As we walked back to the house we began to see the newly blessed candles flicker in the windows of the houses. Men, women, and children, all dressed in white, stood on their porches talking softly, and we hurried home to change. From the path we saw Udi sitting in his wheelchair. Pnina looked at Rina.

"He was wounded in the Yom Kippur War," Rina said.

"I'm sorry."

Pnina was a tall girl who was proud of her height. She held her head erect and wore a bright blue kibbutz hat that perched on her short, dark hair. I remembered then that the small girls on kibbutz imitated her stride and how I had laughed once to watch little Yaffa, Yaakov's sister, practice Pnina's walk with a book balanced on her head.

When Rina introduced Pnina to Udi I saw him study her carefully, but what surprised me was the look of frank interest in her eyes. I knew Pnina had an officer boyfriend. I even knew his name—Ezer. So why was Pnina flashing her green eyes at Udi? Just friendship, I decided and went inside to change into my only white dress which happened to be a tennis dress that luckily had a big hem. I pirouetted in front of the mirror for my friends.

"In this little number I feel equally at home in synagogue or on the courts," I said.

"Lori, stop," Rina said laughing. But she threw me a concerned look, and I realized that Rina knew that I joked the most when I was feeling the worst. I had been thinking of how my grandfather would be getting ready to go alone to the evening service and I wondered whether my parents were back yet from Florida. Whoever heard of a walking trip through the Everglades anyway? You can't hike through a swamp.

We heard Chaim, Esther, and Avraham Macovi leave. They had to be there early because it was Avraham Macovi who sang the Kol Nidre prayer. But Udi was waiting for us downstairs, newly shaven and wearing a white shirt. His dark hair was damp and brushed back, and he was actually smiling.

"Udi!" Rina was pleased. He hadn't gone to synagogue since the war. "You're coming with us?"

"Why not?" He smiled, a smile so like Danni's that he startled me.

We went down the short road together, Pnina and I walking behind Rina and Udi, and we found seats in the last row of the dimly lit synagogue—Udi's chair on the aisle. Avraham Macovi's voice rose strongly in the small room and floated out into the mountain air.

"Kol Nidre," he sang, offering up the ancient prayer that releases man from all vows made during the year past so that a new year may begin free of obligation.

I sat next to Rina and thought that it was wonderful to be offered a chance to begin again each year. Rina's hand reached up to her ring, and I knew that she was thinking of Yaakov who was listening to the same prayer somewhere in Israel's southland. I hoped that Danni, too, had managed to get to a service and, in the last lingering scraps of light, I saw Udi's eyes rest with an unusual softness on Pnina's upturned face.

CHAPTER SEVEN

Pnina stayed on at Balfouria for a couple of days after Yom Kippur, but I didn't see her much. I started classes at the regional high school a couple of miles from the moshav and I really found it tough going. The classes were all taught in Hebrew which I could barely follow in ordinary conversation even after two months in the country, and crash lessons with almost every member of the Eron family except Udi, who would, with a sardonic smile on his face, watch me struggle to read a simple paragraph. The teachers were pretty nice though and found me texts in English and asked me to stay after class so that they could explain anything I didn't understand. I didn't have any problem with math or physics because equations are equations, and luckily the literature course dealt with English and American poets. Emily

Dickinson is very big in Israel and so is Robert Frost. And then too, Rina was in a lot of my classes, and she took meticulous notes and helped explain everything to me in English each night. But it was still a grind, especially after a school like Chatham which, as they liked to say, "relied heavily on verbal communication." That meant that hardly anyone could write a complete sentence.

I stayed up late one night studying, and once or twice I got up from my desk to stretch my legs and glance out the window. On the porch the citronella candle shone with a soft, golden glow, and Pnina and Udi read by its light, their heads very close to each other. Once I thought I saw Udi take her hand and I stepped away from the window very quickly.

When Pnina left she invited us to Sadot HaEmek for the holiday of Sukkot—the festival of booths which commemorates the period during which the children of Israel wandered in the wilderness for forty years before being allowed to enter Canaan under Joshua's leadership.

"Sukkot is beautiful on our kibbutz," Pnina said. "It is the children's favorite holiday. Please come."

"Yes. Why don't you go, girls?" Esther said. "Your grandfather must be at a government meeting in Jerusalem then, and Chaim and I can visit his sister in Tel Aviv."

"But what about Udi?" Rina asked.

I had had the same question but had not asked it because I was prepared for the ultimate in sarcastic answers—something like: "Oh, don't worry about me—I'll go skiing in Lebanon," or "One thing you don't have to think about—and that's my running away."

But instead Udi looked up from the journal he was reading and said, "Didn't I tell you, Rina? I'm going back to Jerusalem. There is a physical therapist at Hadassah Hospital who thinks he can help me, and it's time I was beginning serious work on my dissertation."

Pnina was busy gathering up her index cards when he said that, but I saw the secret smile of satisfaction that crossed her face. It was a familiar smile, and I remembered suddenly how one of the children, I think it was Yaffa, had been working earnestly at some macramé knotting. She kept having difficulty and pleaded with Pnina to help her, but Pnina just looked away; when the child succeeded at last, Pnina smiled that same small smile. Now, however, it made me uneasy. Still, Udi was a grown man. He knew what he was doing, and one thing he absolutely didn't want was advice or insights from me. Besides, he was doing the right thing in going back to Jerusalem. Spine injury or not, he couldn't spend the rest of his life on a front porch in Balfouria.

Rafi and Gad drove us into Acre, stopping at the Nashif house so that I could leave Shalom-Salaam with Nimra. The small camel looked at me mournfully and wouldn't even take the cube of sugar I held out to him. He wasn't fooled. He knew I was abandoning him and going away, and even though I knew I was being ridiculous, my heart sort of cracked when I looked back and saw him limp sadly away.

I forgot about Shalom-Salaam though as we sped toward the kibbutz. Most houses along the road had their own *sukkoth*, small huts covered with branches and decorated with fruits and vegetables, garlands of greenery, and colored paper chains which the children make in school. All of Israel was playing house, and I was not surprised that the children of Sadot HaEmek had built their own little *sukkoth* out of blocks and were decorating them with fruits and vegetables cut from small pieces of colored paper.

Little Yaffa threw her arms around me and quickly grabbed the set of Fisher-Price puppets I'd had my family send for her.

"They are the family for my *sukkah*," she said.

"Oh, Yaffa, share them," another child protested.

"Why should I? They're mine. Lori brought them for me." Yaffa was firm.

"You know, I don't think Yaffa is kibbutz material," I told Pnina.

"It is hard to tell about children," she replied. "One can only give them direction and hope for the best."

It occurred to me that that was what my grandfather had done when he sent me to Israel. Well, he had better add prayers to his hope, I decided.

Every week or so he sent me a money order with some handy aphorism that he picked up from the *Reader's Digest*. "Make the most of this opportunity." "Something learned is something earned." "Procrastination is a thief of time." My grandfather is big on words like "procrastination." But at least he took the time to write something. My parents stuck strictly to a phone call every couple of weeks in which they called me "baby" ten times and kept on asking me to reassure them that I was having a good time.

"I guess you're right," I told Pnina.

"Of course, I'm right." She looked at me as though amazed that I could think her wrong. "Anyway, can you stay with the children now? I want to wash my hair. Ezer is coming this evening."

"Ezer?" I was startled, but Pnina didn't bother answering what really wasn't a question after all. She dashed off and I stayed behind and worked with the children on an enormous mural that showed the two spies carrying bunches of grapes back to . . . I had a . . . of trouble persuading a land . . . kids to paint the grapes purple. The general consensus was in favor of orange.

"But grapes aren't orange," I pointed out.

"In Israel anything can happen," Yaffa retorted. It's very hard arguing with kids who believe in orange grapes, and in the end I wasn't sure that I had been right to dissuade them. Maybe I had dampened their creative urge or something, I thought that it must be wonderful to be like Pnina—always convinced that whatever you did was right. Somehow I always thought that whatever I did was wrong.

That night we ate together in one of the three large *sukkoth* which the kibbutz members had built. The roof was of leaves and straw and filled the large room, constructed from flimsy plywood, with the sweet smell of the fields. Above our heads garlands of oranges and pomegranates swung, intertwined with the branches through which we could see the stars. Rina sat with Yaakov's family, and I shared a table with Amy and Ellen and a large group of volunteers. Their Hebrew was really improving. Amy had picked up the Israeli word *fantasti* which means—oddly enough—fantastic; she replaced "exciting and terrific" with *fantasti*. I think she used the word about fifteen times between the tomato juice and the dessert. They were both feeling pretty cheerful because she'd been transferred out of the laundry and was helping with the harvest.

"I've been in avocados all week," Amy told me proudly, displaying her calluses. "*Fantasti.*" stuck. "It's great," I said and meant it. One thing I missed was working in the greenhouses, but my school schedule didn't give me much chance. Maybe as my Hebrew got better my homework wouldn't pull me down so much, but right now there was no time, and I missed the long quiet hours among the flowers in the moist, fragrant rooms of glass. I had had a chance then to be alone with myself, to begin to understand what I was all about, to piece together things that had happened to me. I felt, during those afternoons of silence, as though I were working out of a giant jigsaw puzzle and the completed picture would tell me who I was and where I was going.

Liesel, the German volunteer, sat across from me, and somehow after dinner we ended up walking out of the *sukkah* together. I liked the tall, blond girl whose eyes always seemed just a little bit sad. Of all the volunteers who had arrived together, Liesel's Hebrew was the best, and Pnina had told me that she was the hardest worker and always volunteered for the hardest jobs. As we walked out, one of the children gave us each a branch of the myrtle leaves which had been gathered for the holiday.

"This is a beautiful holiday, is it not?" Liesel asked.

"I like harvest holidays," I agreed.

"But this is different from the other harvest festivals. It does not celebrate a harvest that has been but one that will be. It doesn't give thanks for rains that have fallen, but it prays for rains that will fall. It is a festival of hope; hope for a better, more bountiful world; hope for a more peaceful future." Liesel spoke in English and her voice was deadly earnest. When I looked at her I was surprised to see her china blue eyes bright with unshed tears which she made no move to hide.

"That is all we can do," she said, more to herself than to me. "We must work and pray for a more peaceful future."

She peeled her myrtle branch, and we sniffed at its sharp, swift fragrance.

"But that's what you are doing, Liesel," I said, knowing that I must try to comfort her although I was oddly certain that I could not.

"I try," she said simply and turned off to walk alone down a different path.

That night Rina told me that Liesel was a high school student when she first learned about World War II and what had happened to the Jews in the concentration camps. When she asked her family about it her father told her he had worked at a camp in Poland. He had been a young soldier and had only followed orders. When she asked what sort of orders, he did not answer her, but that night she heard him call out fearfully in his sleep and she thought she understood what his orders had been. He had wept when she told her family she was going to Israel to work, but he had not tried to discourage her, and she had spent three summers in Israel before coming to spend the year.

"Do you think she will stay here?" I asked.

"Perhaps, but I'm not sure. What is important is that she is here now," Rina said. "Stop thinking of everything in such a long term way, Lori." She fingered the ring that hung about her neck, and I knew that Rina was annoyed because she did not want to think about the future, about the day when she would have to tell her father, Chaim Eron, about Yaakov Gamliel whose skin shimmered like coal. But I wanted to think about the future. I didn't want to wake up one day the way my mother had, and realize that what I wanted, after all, was a different sort of life from the one I had. And I didn't want to run from playground to playground, the way my parents did, trying to find an excitement, a satisfaction that somehow they always missed.

I wrote a letter to Danni that night, telling him about Sukkot on the kibbutz, Shalom-Salaam's leg, which was healing so well, and how pleased everyone was with Udi's decision to go to Jerusalem. I didn't say anything about Pnina and I didn't say anything about the way I thought about Danni when the night air became soft and the stars seemed to leap down at me as I looked at them. It was a nice, serious letter from a nice, serious girl who spent a lot of time doing her homework. Then I wrote a letter to my grandfather telling him about Yom Kippur at Balfouria and asking him (just so he shouldn't think I was sick) for some extra money in case Danni and I needed it for our Chanukah trip. I wrote a letter to my parents also, asking them for a lot of junk I didn't need, complaining about the food and about how there was only one television station in

Israel. Then I looked at the three sealed envelopes and said softly, "Will the real Lori Mandell please stand up?"

"What?" Rina murmured lazily from the depths of her sleep.

"Nothing," I said, but there was no reason to answer: Rina had turned over on her back and slept now with a beautiful smile on her face, her fingers entwined about the chain on which Yaakov's ring dangled.

The next day Yaffa took me to the Gamliel's small bungalow. It was the first time I had been there and I looked around curiously. Like the other small houses that were assigned to married couples on the kibbutz, it had a small sitting room, a bedroom, and a tiny kitchen furnished with a hot plate and a two-shelf refrigerator. The wooden floors were covered with bright, woven rugs of the unique Falasha weave, and several gay pillows of similar patterns were scattered on the sofa.

Mrs. Gamliel, a small woman who smiled a great deal, showed us through the little house, even demonstrating that water actually flowed from the kitchen faucets.

"Oh, Ima," little Yaffa cried out in exasperation. "It's just water."

"Yaffa does not know what it was like to grow up in a country where all the water had to be carried from the well in jugs. To me, every day in this country is a miracle."

"Then let us thank God for the miracle."

Yaakov's father had come in quietly, and he, too, looked around the small house with pride. I remembered the way Avraham Macovi surveyed Balfouria each morning. He would have no trouble understanding the Gamliels.

Mr. Gamliel's curly beard quivered when he talked and his eyes flashed. I had never seen his hands still. They darted about, fixing things, pointing to things or drawing in small flashing movements. Now he held a *lulav*, a palm branch surrounded on each side with branches of willow and myrtle, and an *etrog*, the lovely lemony fruit of the citron tree.

"Come, we will make the prayer of the season," he said and put the *lulav* and the *etrog* in Yaffa's hand. It was Liesel who explained to me that Jews everywhere repeated the prayer, praying together for a good harvest.

"But I think it goes beyond Jews," the German girl had said gravely. "I think all people must pray together for a good harvest."

Now I watched as Mr. Gamliel asked Yaffa to repeat the prayer thanking God for the privilege of blessing His fruits. Gently, he taught the child to point the *lulav* and *etrog* slowly in all four directions and up and down.

"Why does he do that?" I whispered to Rina who had come quietly into the room.

"It is to show that God is everywhere," Rina answered. I wondered if Liesel knew that and I felt a sudden sadness for the lovely blond girl who had spent her youth struggling to make amends for a crime that was not her own.

"Rina, when do you go back to Balfouria?" Mrs. Gamliel asked, setting the table for tea.

"Tomorrow morning. We have to be at school," Rina answered.

"I have made a pillow as a gift for your parents, and my husband has carved your father an ashtray in the Amharic design. Will you bring them as gifts?"

An uncomfortable silence filled the room. Slowly, Mrs. Gamliel circled the table pouring the tea, but the unanswered question hovered in the air. It was Yaakov's father who broke the silence.

"Rina and Lori have much to carry with them this time. They take back grapes and pomegranates, and Yaffa has dates for them from the children's farm. Perhaps next time, when their arms are freer, they will carry our gifts back to Rina's home," he said.

Before another silence could descend I spotted Yaakov's guitar in a corner and seized it.

"Say, Yaffa, do you know this song?"

I struck up "Old MacDonald Had a Farm," which she cheerfully sang in Hebrew, turning Old MacDonald into a character called *Dod Moshe* (Uncle Moshe), and as she sang her mother danced, a lovely swaying circle dance that our small group joined in with me still strumming away. Rina left after that, but I stayed on. The Gamliels taught me two songs that they had sung in Ethiopia, and I plucked at chords until they told me I had caught it. Someone should write that music down, I thought, and I wondered if we could stop at a store in Acre and pick up a couple of music notebooks.

"Lori, why is it that Rina does not take our gifts to her parents, that we do not meet them?" Mrs. Gamliel asked me as I was leaving.

"I guess she just thinks it's a little too soon," I said and I was relieved when no one asked "too soon for what?" because I didn't know myself.

We had another *kumsitz* that night at which Amy made the pronouncement that Sukkot at Sadot HaEmek was *fantasti*, and two South African boys taught us a song called "Hold 'Em Down the Zulu Warrior." We were still singing it as we walked home, and I was glad I was walking with Liesel and not with Rina when we passed the children's house. Someone's flashlight trapped Phina and Ezer in a circle of light. The tall soldier's arms were around her, and her dark head rested on his shoulder. I thought of the letter in Udi's handwriting that I had seen on Phina's bed that morning. I wondered why my heart should sink that way when Udi and I weren't exactly friends.

"What did you say? I'm sorry." Liesel had been talking, but I hadn't listened.

"Nothing important. Just that the sky is very beautiful tonight."

"Yes, it is."

We looked up together and stared at the silvery stars that drifted lazily through nets of night-dark clouds. A sudden wind blew and I shivered. Fall had begun and soon winter would be here. We walked more quickly then, as though, mysteriously, we were losing precious time.

CHAPTER EIGHT

The weeks after Sukkot were gray and rainy. We awoke every morning to the gray mist that spilled down over Balfouria from the mountains of Lebanon. A pale, silvery sunlight slipped across the sky as we drove to school in the moshav pickup truck, but by afternoon a slow steady rainfall would begin. Sometimes I got the feeling that I would never be completely dry or warm again.

"But in America the winter and fall must be much colder than here," Rina pointed out when I complained.

"Yeah, but in America we have this super invention called central heating. When you walk inside a house or a building you're actually warm."

I huddled closer to the little kerosene heater whose a bright but very limited blaze gave out what I knew, must be heat because sometimes

Rina and I made toast on its grill. I was feeling particularly bitchy that afternoon because two weeks had gone by without a letter from Danni. I knew that he was doing paratroop training somewhere, and when I was feeling optimistic I reasoned with myself that he couldn't write letters while floating through the sky. But when I was feeling brutally realistic I reminded myself that no one, not even the most dedicated recruit in the Israeli army, spent twenty-four hours a day tumbling out of airplanes. Surely he could have found five minutes to write one of his more meaningful messages like "Hope you are practicing your Hebrew" or "How is Shalom-Salaam's leg?" The only mail I did get was from Marcie who thought that the blouse of kaffiyah material I had sent her was "super"; she wore it without a bra just to get a rise out of Dr. Chalmers. The big thing at Chatham this year was "learning through seeing." The kids in economics were taking tours of factories and the stock market. A Christmas trip to Spain was planned for the Spanish students, and one to France was scheduled for the French students. Marcie had registered for an elective in the "Judeo-Christian Tradition" because she'd heard that there was talk of a trip to Jerusalem for the kids registered in that course. She thought that that would give her a chance to meet those Israeli soldiers I'd written her about who looked like Paul Newman. I also got a letter from my grandfather telling me that "the seeds of the present were the crops of the future," which meant that I should study now so that I could get into a decent college later. He enclosed an advertisement for one of my father's showroom sales which showed my father giving thousand-watt blow driers to twin teen-agers with long, blond hair. I was grateful that my father wasn't drying their hair, although I knew that he and my mother probably had matching driers and screamed over their noise while they played beauty parlor. I didn't show the picture to the Erons. I was pretty sure that I knew what they would think of it.

I burned the ad and in the heater, glad that Rina was involved in a letter to Yaakov and wasn't paying any attention to me. Unlike Danni, Yaakov wrote every day, and Rina picked up the mail herself so that her parents wouldn't see the letters. But once or twice I'd noticed Esther Eron look in the door as Rina was bent over a letter to Yaakov, and just the other day I saw her at the window watching as Rina walked back from the mailbox, absorbed in Yaakov's letter. I wondered if Rina had forgotten that her mother had once been an intelligence agent for the Haganah.

Esther called up to me just then that Nimra had arrived, and I dashed down, glad to leave our room. It wasn't that I begrudged Rina Yaakov's literary devotion—I just wanted a postcard of my own telling me to stay warm.

Nimra and I settled down with our books at the dining room table. Nimra was taking the entrance exams for the Hebrew University Faculty of Agriculture in a couple of months' time, and I'd offered to help her with her English. Sometimes though, I got the feeling I was learning more Arabic than she was picking up English. That afternoon, for instance, she kept mixing up adverbs and adjectives so that her sentences tumbled out like "Chlorophyll makes grass greenly." I thought the examiner would be impressed by her knowledge, but I had to point out that there wasn't a word like "greenly."

"What's the matter today, Nimra?" I asked. "You were doing better last week."

She glanced over to the kitchen where Esther was jarring jam made from the citrons. Their sweet lemony odor filled the room, and Esther's face was flushed with the heat. As she sealed a jar Chaim walked into the room behind her, took her face in his hands, and gently kissed her. I didn't know why watching that kiss should make me feel so sad, but as I followed Nimra out of the room I knew that I was pretty close to crying. Maybe it was all that darn rain or maybe it was the sudden memory of my mother and father sitting very close to each other on the small, wicker loveseat in our Vineyard house. They were listening to the end of the Sunday symphony, their heads touching, their fingers intertwined, while I sat at their feet doing a jigsaw puzzle. I didn't have too many memories like that and I was glad I had dredged this one up. I knew now why I felt like crying. I was homesick. Pure and simple. I missed my mommy and daddy. Somehow that realization made me feel happy. After all, if I were homesick, that meant I had a home—something I hadn't always been too sure of.

"What is it, Lori?" Nimra asked when we were alone at last in the barn with Shalom-Salaam eating dried barley grass from my hand.

"I was just about to ask you the same thing," I said. "You haven't exactly been yourself this lesson."

Nimra sighed and pulled her long, black sweater closed over the heavy, embroidered purple dress that constituted fifty percent of her wardrobe—the other half being a dark skirt and white blouse that had been the convent's contribution to high fashion. Rina and I were going to have to get her outfitted for Rehovoth somehow or other.

"I think maybe I should not bother with the lessons. It is all a dream, that I can study at a university."

"Why is it a dream? Avraham Macovi says that your scholarship is a cinch. Your grades at the convent school were terrific, and even your English isn't so badly."

"Bad," she said with a weak smile.

"See? I couldn't correct myself in Hebrew like that. Your English is much better than my Hebrew."

"Not a very great compliment," she pointed out.

"All right. Let's stop playing. What's really the matter?"

"My father is very opposed to my going. He

says that the place of an Arab woman is in the home. He says if I become too educated I will have difficulty finding a husband. Also he does not think it good that I will be studying mostly with Jews. He did not object to the convent because there almost all the students were Arab girls."

"But isn't this a switch for him?" I asked, puzzled. "Avraham Macovi has been over this with him again and again. There are other Arab students at the Faculty of Agriculture. Your mother has told him she can manage the house without you. And your father certainly isn't against the Jews. He and Avraham Macovi are good friends."

"He has been much influenced by my cousin Ibrahim," Nimra said.

"Your cousin? But I thought your whole family had left the country—that you had no relations here?" Nimra had told me that during the fighting in 1948, when the Arab armies attacked the newborn state of Israel, almost all her relatives had crossed the border into Lebanon. Her father, who had personal assurances from Avraham Macovi, had tried to persuade them to stay, but they refused to listen to him. They were certain that the Israelis would take over their houses and burn their crops if they won, although they didn't really think that that was possible. The Arab chieftains had advised them to leave without even taking any of their possessions. When they returned they would have their pick of the houses of the Jews who would have been herded into the sea. Some of them left with their laundry still dangling on the clotheslines to be plucked off when they returned. Others simply tethered their small animals and left them two or three days' supply of food and water, because they were sure that they would be back. The Israeli radio begged them to stay, and light planes flew over the Arab villages dropping mimeographed leaflets telling the Arabs that all the new state of Israel wanted was for all its citizens to live together in peace. But the voices of the chieftains in Beirut and Damascus were louder, and only Abdul Nashif of all the Arabs in that area had remained.

Nimra gave me a startled look and turned away, but I saw the blood rush to her cheeks.

"You must not mention that I told you this," she said softly, and again her eyes avoided mine. "I was just feeling so very bad that it slipped out—the name of my cousin."

"He came across the border from Lebanon?" I asked.

She nodded.

"But not to do any mischief. Only to visit the grave of his mother and to bring greetings to my family. Ibrahim is a good boy, a gentle boy. He will be gone after tomorrow."

"Your father is doing a dangerous thing in harboring him," I said. "It was the rule in Israel that the houses of those who gave refuge to infiltrators from the Arab countries could be destroyed.

"Ibrahim is not a terrorist," Nimra said indignantly. "He is a gentle person, the father of many children."

"All right," I said, but I wasn't convinced. Liesel's father, who had worked in a concentration camp in Poland, was a popular chemistry teacher and grew roses.

"You won't say anything then?" Nimra pleaded.

"I can't talk about something I don't know anything about," I said. "But he ought to leave, Nimra. Right away."

"You are right."

She pulled her sweater up over her head, patted Shalom-Salaam on the head, and hurried out.

I stayed on in the barn for a few minutes brushing my little camel who really wasn't so little anymore.

"Did I do the right thing, Shalom-Salaam?" I asked softly. One of the first rules of the Chatham School was never to rat on anyone, but there was a big difference between setting bombs in supermarkets and smoking pot in the locker room. But there, I was doing it again—overdramatizing myself. Nimra's cousin had just come to visit his mother's grave.

"Right, Shalom-Salaam?" I asked as I left, and my camel nodded solemnly and turned his attention to more important things like barley grass.

As I walked back to the house I caught a glimpse of an army jeep parked right in front.

"Danni," I thought and began running. That

was why he hadn't written for so long—he had been planning a visit.

But it was the uniformed arms of Pnina's officer-friend Ezer that I ran into.

"Lori," he said, "Shalom, what's the hurry?"

"I'm sorry," I said, and my face felt very hot. "I thought you were someone else."

"Well, I'm sorry I'm not." He laughed. "Pnina asked me to drop some things off here on my way north."

"On your way north? You can't get much further north," I said.

"Oh, I have to go almost to the border. There's been some talk of infiltrators. It's probably just rumor, but after Maalot we're not taking any chances."

At the word "infiltrators" I thought again of Nimra's cousin Ibrahim. My heart stood still, and again I wrestled with myself. What if I were wrong and Ibrahim had not crossed the border merely to visit his parents' graves? I should tell Ezer about him, I knew, but I had promised Nimra. Promised her and accepted her thanks. And Ezer had said it was just rumor. After Maalot there had been a tightening of security, and an electrified fence had been built around the Lebanese border. Surely, that would contain any terrorists. But even as I struggled to reassure myself, a sick feeling grabbed me. No matter what I did, I would be wrong.

"Can anyone get in through the fence?" I asked.

"Isn't it electronically wired to send off warnings or something?"

"There are ways," Ezer said. "Anyway I left the packages with Rina's mother. Will I see you at Sadot HaEmek at Chanukah?"

"I'm going to Jerusalem, I think," I replied, thinking that I'd be going to Jerusalem if Danni Eron remembered who I was.

"All right then. Shalom," Ezer said. "I want to get to the border before nightfall."

"Take care," I said, and Ezer tossed me a snappy salute. As his jeep pulled away I could hear his transistor radio playing "Yellow Submarine," which seemed a stupid song for a soldier on his way to a border mission to be listening to.

In the kitchen Esther was looking admiringly at a handknit, gaily striped woolen scarf. I recognized the bright red, yellow, and green pattern at once. Pnina had been working on it when we were at the kibbutz on Sukkot.

"She sent it for Udi. His grandfather will take it to him when he goes to Jerusalem tomorrow. Isn't that thoughtful of her?"

"Yeah," I said unenthusiastically. What was Pnina doing anyway—sending Ezer with a handknit gift for Udi? It reminded me of the time Marcie had asked one guy she was dating from the Calhoun School to pick up tickets for a concert she wanted to go to with a senior at Chatham. But Marcie had been fifteen then; Pnina had finished army service and her master's degree. She was too old for such stupid games. The whole thing depressed me, and I wasn't even cheered up when Esther gave me the drawings Yaffa had made for me and the small scarf of Yaakov's mother's distinctive weave.

"What lovely work. Who wove that?" Esther asked, bending over the colorful fabric.

"An Ethiopian woman on the kibbutz," I said, and I didn't look up because I knew Rina was standing in the doorway, a mute plea in her eyes.

I was getting tired of being the keeper of so many secrets and I was glad that I'd be spending that evening with Rafi and Gad working on an arrangement of some songs a Bukharian family at Balfouria had taught us. The pages of my new music notebooks were getting filled pretty fast. It was a good session, and I came home feeling pretty good. We'd worked up a terrific harmony. I was singing it when I came into the Eron parlor, but I stopped when Avraham Macovi put his hands to my lips.

The whole family was clustered around the radio, and a newscaster was shooting out bulletins so fast that I could hardly make out a single sentence.

"What happened?" I asked.

Avraham Macovi switched the radio off and sighed deeply.

"A bomb was planted on the bus to Nahariya. Fortunately, a soldier on the bus noticed a strangely shaped box, and when he saw what it was he threw himself out of the bus with the bomb. He was killed. His body shattered. Nineteen years old."

We were all quiet, offering the unknown boy our silence. I thought of the slender soldiers who had taught me the Hebrew words to "Where Have All the Flowers Gone?" "Gone to graveyards, every one." The refrain haunted me, and for the second time that day I felt tears stirring. I should have told someone about Nimra's cousin. Probably he had nothing to do with it, but still, I should have said something.

"At a garage not far from here they found a cache of other weapons—some very similar to that bomb. We must watch carefully for any strangers."

Chaim Eron locked the doors and windows very carefully that night, even checking the buildings, and Rina took a flashlight up to our room with her.

"Lori," she asked when we were in bed, "what was bothering Nimra today? I saw her running when she left the barn."

"I don't know," I said and closed my eyes. The rhythms of the Bukharian tune stirred in my mind, and I got out of bed to make a note. I sat by the window writing in a shaft of moonlight, and when I was through I looked out into the velvety darkness of the night. Our window faced the Nashif house, and I saw a sudden flicker of light, a slender beam piercing the blackness. Swiftly I pulled the shade and hurried back to bed, shivering with a chill that had nothing to do with the mountain winds that streaked down across Balfouria from the north.

CHAPTER NINE

It snows in Israel. I really expected it to. After all, all that the [gover]nment Tourist Office commercials show are people skin diving in Eilat o[r] picking flowers in the Sharon Valley; but then I hadn't ever expected it to be cold and damp either. We woke up one November morning and a thin curtain of snow glistened across Avraham Macovi's citron trees and coated the pebbled paths. I opened the window and licked the clean snow that clung to the sill, remembering how my father used to gather snow in paper cups and mix it with chocolate syrup.

"What are you doing?" Rina asked lazily, still half-asleep.

"I'm making a sundae. Want a taste?" I held a snow-covered finger out to her, and she jumped out of bed.

"Snow!" she shouted.

"That lovely lady has identified the mystery object. Give her a year's supply of toilet paper and a subscription to the popular evening newspaper, *Maariv*," I said, but then I saw the look of wonder that had settled on Rina's face. "What's the matter? Haven't you ever seen snow before?" I asked.

"Oh, on the mountaintops. And three years ago there was a small snowfall but only for one or two hours. Nothing like this." She too traced her finger across the snow and held it up to her lips. "I wish Yaakov was in the north. He has never seen snow at all."

"I'll get my camera. We'll take pictures of it," I said. I wasn't serious, but Rina thought that it was a great idea; and after breakfast the whole family put on hats and coats, and we all photographed each other standing next to the snow-laden trees. It was a real event for most of Israel—the three inches that fell that day. As we drove to school we saw other families posing for photos, and that night Avraham Macovi took down his photo album and showed us snapshots of other snowfalls during his years in Israel. There hadn't been too many, but one of the pictures showed a cluster of tents nestled in the citron orchard, and the branches of the trees were covered with lacy leaves of ice.

"This was during our second winter in Bal-fouria. When it snowed then, the canvas of the tents leaked. The Nashif clan—there were many Nashifs in the area then—came and offered us shelter, and for the three days of the snow we slept in their houses. Abdul's father was the chief then. He died just before the war in 'forty-eight. I often think that if he had been alive then, our neighbors would not have fled; that we could have lived together peacefully." Avraham Macovi's voice was pensive, and his words came slowly, the way my grandfather's did when he talked of his youth in Germany.

"Who became chief after the old man died?" Rina asked. "Not Abdul?"

"No. His older brother."

"Was he Ibrahim's father?" I asked.

Esther shot me a swift, surprised look.

"How do you know of Ibrahim?" she asked. "He left the country when he was a small boy—in 'forty-eight."

"Oh, Nimra sometimes talks about her cousins," I said quickly, and I was relieved when Esther turned back to the album because my hands were shaking and I knew that the blood was rushing to my face. That's always been my problem. I'm a lousy liar. As an intelligence agent I'd probably be a big zero.

We looked at a series of photos of Avraham Macovi growing older, his woolen hat crowned by the snowfall of 'forty-three, the snowfall of 'forty-nine, and the big snow of the late fifties—at least five inches that paralyzed all highway traffic in the northern Galilee. It was sort of a picture history of Balfouria.

That night as Rina wrote Yaakov a ten-page letter about the snow (I mean what is there to say about snow anyway—that it's white and cold and sometimes soft and it freezes into ice? Being in love must mean being able to fill up ten pages on snow.), I thought about how Balfouria had grown from a stretch of desolate land, reclaimed from the swamp to the thriving settlement blanketed with fertile fields and gardens. I thought dreamily, then, about going off to some barren strip of land and cultivating it—watching young shoots of green struggle forth. Yaakov and Rina talked about starting a new kibbutz with a group of other kids when they finished their army service. It had always seemed like a crazy idea, but now it sounded like a good and wonderful life. I'd work alongside someone who looked mysteriously like Danni and we'd sing. I even got the words of the song and the melody—

"Oh to be young then
And close to the earth . . ."

I began singing it and realized that the Brothers Four had gotten to that song before I had.

"Oh well," I thought, "that's show biz."

I looked at Rina, still bent over her letter, and I took up my pad.

"Dear Danni," I wrote. "It snowed today and it was very beautiful. I miss you. Why don't you write to me?"

I mailed it without stopping to think what Marcie would have said about a letter like that. But she would have been wrong, because a week later I had a three-page letter—and two pages were devoted to our Chanukah trip to Jerusalem.

By the time I got Danni's letter the snow had melted, but Esther was still worried about the Nashif family. She was sure that they weren't prepared for such cold weather, and she packed up a parcel of warm clothing and extra blankets and asked Rina and myself to take it over. Rina begged off because she was working in the greenhouse. The cold had screwed up the heating controls, and we'd lost a fair amount of gladioli and tulips. So I went alone. Rafi drove me over and agreed to pick me up in another hour.

I hadn't seen Nimra since she'd told me about her cousin Ibrahim. Twice when we had lessons scheduled, she'd sent one of her younger brothers over to cancel them, with excuses about being busy or sick. I hadn't believed her, and I knew that she hadn't expected me to believe her. I didn't even try to make another date. But Danni had asked specifically about Nimra in his letter and even given me the names of some books he wanted her to read.

I knocked at the door of the small stone house and realized that although I'd visited Nimra and her family several times, we had always sat outside. I had never been inside the small stone house.

It was Hulda Nashif, Nimra's mother, who opened the door and asked me at once to come in. The large room was lit by a single electric bulb that dangled from the ceiling, but a real fire blazed in a stone fireplace. The walls were lined with couches covered with woven spreads, and I realized that at night the couches were taken apart to make up beds for the family. The kitchen furnishings were a couple of kerosene stoves and an ancient ice box which had been painted a bright blue. The smaller children knelt on scatter rugs on the floor, playing with small animals carved out of olive wood, and Nimra sat on a soft leather hassock, an open book on her lap. She smiled at me shyly and quickly tucked her book underneath the skirt of her purple dress.

I handed the parcel to Hulda, and through elaborate sign language we managed to get it understood that she would be honored to make me a cup of coffee and I would be honored to drink it. Then I walked over to Nimra and pulled up the hassock opposite her and sat down.

"I am glad to see you," she said.

"Aha, you've been studying your English," I replied.

"What do you mean?"

"Well, you didn't say 'gladly to see you.'"

She smiled but shook her head.

"I haven't been studying," she said. "I've decided not to take the examination."

"That's ridiculous." I fished Danni's letter out. "Here are the names of some books Danni wants you to read." I read out the titles and was glad I didn't want to go to Agriculture school. I didn't particularly want to curl up on a winter night with a text on plant morphology or a gripping analysis of desert soil.

"Listen," I said, adopting the offhand tone Marcie used when she made believe she really didn't care but was trying really hard to convince me of something—a trick she probably picked up from her shrink father. "You can just take the exam. You don't have to go on to the university. But don't you at least want the satisfaction of knowing you could get in if you wanted to? That's worth something." I didn't know what it was worth, and I was glad Nimra didn't ask. "And you have so been studying." I pointed to the botany text that had slid to the floor.

"Where would I get the books?" Nimra asked, and I knew I had won. I also knew I had the answer.

"I'm going to Tel Aviv tomorrow for the Thanksgiving dinner at the ZOA House. Why don't you come along? Rina's going, too. They asked us to bring guests."

"Thanksgiving?" Nimra asked. There is no "th" sound in Arabic, and the word tumbled out with a sibilant "s" that sounded so good that I decided to adopt it.

"An American holiday. Come on. The pickup is going in from Balfouria, so we don't even have to worry about transportation. Ask your mother."

Nimra threw me a big-eyed look, as though begging me to forget an invitation she was clearly having a difficult time turning down, but I stood my ground. That's one advantage in being a spoiled, only child—you learn how to wear people down. Finally, she went off to consult with her mother. I knew that it was all right because Hulda Nashif was flashing me a big gold-toothed smile when she came in with my cup of sweet, hot Arab coffee. We nodded happily at each other, all three of us, and I told Nimra we'd pick her up at seven. I had just enough time to gulp down my coffee before Rafi was back to take me home to Balfouria. When I reported my invitation and Nimra's acceptance to Esther and Rina they looked at each other in astonishment.

"I don't think Nimra's ever been to Tel Aviv," Esther said. "I certainly know Hulda hasn't."

"You see, things are changing. The Arabs have new feelings about sharing in the life of Israel. We will yet be able to live together. This is a fine thing you did, Lori," Avraham Macovi said.

I didn't answer. I wondered what Avraham Macovi would think if he knew about my conversation with Nimra in the barn, and I was glad he left to answer the phone just then because I knew I'd have a hard time looking him in the eye.

We drove southward the next day through the mist that drifted down from the mountains and over the newly gleaned fields. Then we rolled down the Haifa Road and sniffed the sharp, acrid scent of the Mediterranean and strained to catch a glimpse of the blue ribbon of ocean that licked at the pink sands of the shoreline. Children along the road waved to us, and south of Haifa we picked up two girl-soldiers who waved their thanks, climbed in the back, and continued chatting as though we weren't there. One of them was getting married when she finished her army service, and she took swathes of white fabric out of her kit bag.

"What do you think of this for the dress?" she asked her friend, holding up a piece of sheer organdy.

"Too flimsy," the other girl replied and reached for a swatch of creamy satin. She took off her maroon army beret and fashioned a Juliet cap from the scrap of material. "There," she said, satisfied, and we turned to look at her, the soldier briefly become a bride.

I took up my guitar and sang, "I never will marry; I'll be no man's wife; I intend to stay single all the days of my life. . . ."

Gad and Rafi laughed and took up the refrain, and Rina translated the song for the soldiers and Nimra who also tried it. We were laughing and singing as the pickup truck rolled through Ramat Gan with its neat little suburban houses and then down to Tel Aviv where we could see the outline of the tall buildings and hear the increased hum of noise as the road grew more crowded with cars and small clusters of people waited impatiently at each crossing. Nimra looked out, fascinated at the plate-glass store windows with their colorful displays, the wide streets, the canopied cafes with their bright little tables at which people sipped coffees even though the weather was cold enough so that some of them even wore thick, wool gloves as they drank. We dropped the soldiers off at Dizengoff Street and watched them disappear into a bridal accessory shop. I decided that I definitely would not write Marcie about them. There was something decidedly unmilitary about soldiers who debated the virtues of organdy-versus satin. But then, I might be talking to Marcie about them. Her last letter had said that it looked as though the students of the Judeo-Christian Tradition were going to make it to Jerusalem that winter—at least they had all threatened to drop the course if a trip wasn't thrown in.

We parked the truck near the Helena Rubinstein Art Museum and walked on, passing through a strange little park called Gan Yaakov where trees and shrubbery seemed to be running a winning race with cement walks and benches. Kids were climbing all around, and their mothers were watching them, wearing the same bored, stoic looks that the Central Park mothers wore when I used to pass them on my way to Chatham. Mothers are mothers, I decided, thinking that that could be my Profundity of the Week. Except mine, I added, mentally. My mother, after all, was a hotshot lawyer, a consumer advocate, and a Washington Personality. Even *Time* magazine had said so. She wouldn't be caught dead sitting under a tree, either in Central Park or in Gan Yaakov.

"See this tree," Rina said, pointing to a tall, ancient sycamore that threw its velvety shadow over half the park. "My grandfather told me that when he was a young man, before the park was built, people from the neighborhood used to bring their camels here to relax in the shade."

I looked at the speeding cars and swift cyclists, the running children and their tired, patient mothers. No, I definitely could not imagine Shalom-Salaam relaxing in the pool of shade which was currently shared by almost a dozen toddlers playing a variation of ring-around-a-rosy.

The entry hall of the ZOA House was already crowded, and the Israeli guards glanced at the groups of Americans and their guests with interest. It was strange to realize that all of Israel was having an ordinary workday while we Americans were clinging to a reenactment of a piece of our history that had taken place more than two hundred years ago in prerevolutionary Massachusetts. The massive building was permeated with the odors of the holiday—roasting turkeys, stuffing laced with onions and sage—and someone had even managed to find cranberries because their tart odor drifted over the room. Everyone sniffed appreciatively. I guess that we were glad to smell those aromas of home and to know that even if we weren't in San Francisco or Evanston or New York, we were sharing the experience of our families who were.

"Back home we always had creamed broccoli at Thanksgiving. No one really liked it, and we never had it any other time during the year, but somehow it was always on the table at Thanksgiving and we always ate it," a cute red-headed girl wearing a bright pink happy-face sweat shirt said.

Amy and Ellen waved wildly to us from across the room, and I saw that Pnina was with them. I introduced them to Rafi and Gad, and I knew that I wouldn't have to worry about any of them for the rest of the day. Rafi was talking rapidly, and Ellen greeted everything he said with a staccato chorus of *fantastis*.

"How's Ezer?" I asked Pnina.

"Oh, he is fine. In the south now. And I had a wonderful letter from Udi. I must tell Rina." She ploughed through the crowd looking for Rina just as I was about to ask her what kind of game she was playing. Oh well, it really wasn't any of my business, and Udi surely wouldn't thank me for my interest. I turned to Nimra and began telling her the Thanksgiving story and explaining the crayoned drawings that the kids from the American School at Herzliah had drawn for the building.

She already knew about the Indians being there when the Pilgrims arrived and how America had originally belonged to them. But she didn't know a thing about how the Indians had helped the Pilgrims and taught them to plant maize or how they had celebrated together in the cleared forests of the land that they would share.

"It is something like the Arabs and the Jews here," she said thoughtfully and I nodded. The parallels were so obvious that I really had been an idiot not to recognize them—I who had always gotten top grades in social studies.

"We helped the Jews when they first came," Nimra continued. "That is, some of us helped some of the Jews. Others fought them."

"It worked that way back in Massachusetts, too," I said, asserting myself as one of Chatham's top social studies scholars.

"And now in your country—are all things shared between the Indians and the others?" she asked.

"No," I said regretfully, thinking of the poverty on the Indian reservation I had visited the last time I was in Florida with my father. "That takes time, lots of time." That was what my father had said, and I had to accept his answer because there didn't seem to be any other, although I thought that three centuries was really plenty of time.

"That is what my father told my cousin Ibrahim," she said softly.

I didn't answer because I didn't want to hear any more about her cousin Ibrahim. Nimra must have read my thoughts because she pressed my hand.

"Lori," she said, "He will not come again. My father has told him that he cannot—that our home is not open to him."

"I'm glad," I said and felt as though a weight had been lifted from my heart. "Listen Nimra, the way to make things happen more quickly is for everyone to do what they can. And what you can do is go to the university."

She looked at me, her dark eyes troubled, and

then she looked at a drawing of an Indian boy and a Pilgrim boy seeding a field together.

"I will talk to my father again," she said.

We walked into the dining room together. The American School chorus was on stage singing "We Gather Together to Ask the Lord's Blessing" which was followed by the Savyon School's rendition in Hebrew of "How Good It is for Brethren to Dwell Together." We found seats with Rina, Pnina, Amy and Rafi, and Ellen and Gad, and over the sound of the singing I could hear Ellen's ringing *fantasti* and Pnina's serious voice telling Rina that Udi had written her to say that he was walking with crutches now.

The turkey was delicious, and we spent the rest of the afternoon wandering around Tel Aviv, remembering to stop at a bookstore for Nimra's texts. It was late at night when we got to Balfouria, and Esther was waiting on the porch for us.

"Just in time, Lori," she said. "Your father is on the telephone."

I dashed in, suddenly very glad that he had called, that he had remembered me on the holiday.

"Happy Thanksgiving," he said.

"Happy Thanksgiving, Daddy," I replied. "Gee, holidays are terrific, aren't they?"

"Yes," he said, after a minute. "They are." I got the feeling that he somehow knew that what I meant was that it was important that there were special days that drew people closer—that reminded friends and family of who they were and where they belonged. He asked me, during that call, if there was anything special I needed because Marcie would be coming to Israel with her class. I couldn't think of anything, and when I hung up I stood alone in the kitchen for a minute and looked out the window at the dark sky hung with wintry stars. December was going to be a very busy month.

CHAPTER TEN

I stood on the corner of King George Road and Ben Yehudah Street in Jerusalem and shivered even though I was wearing my hooded, plaid winter coat and three sweaters underneath it. A vendor, pushing an enormous aluminum cart from which steam poured, stopped, looked at me hopefully, and pointed to his merchandise which consisted of golden ears of corn and baked potatoes packed tightly together across glowing coals. I gave him ten *grush* and took a potato which I did not want to eat but couldn't resist clutching. He smiled a toothless, old man's smile, and continued down the hill shouting mournfully into the wind. I held my potato tightly and trailed after him wishing that I hadn't decided to come to Jerusalem a week ahead of Danni. Being alone in the city of peace was destroying my self-image as Independent, Self-Reliant Lori. Still, it had seemed silly to stay on alone at Balfouria after my winter exams were finished, and I really felt that I owed myself a present for getting grades that were bound to impress even Dr. Chalmers who didn't believe in grades. (When they saw my "excellent" in physics, they'd pay me to go to Chatham.) I hadn't wanted to go to Sadot HaEmek with Rina because I didn't want to answer the mute question in Yaakov's mother's eyes and because I didn't want to see Pnina. I had decided to take a vacation from secrets.

It had been Avraham Macovi who had solved the problem of where I would stay by arranging for me to board at a hostel for foreign students in the outskirts of the city near Mount Herzl.

"The only thing is that they are quite strict there. You must be in your room by eleven because they lock the front door then. But that is not very difficult because the last bus leaves the city at ten-thirty, and it is only a fifteen-minute ride," he said.

That curfew really hadn't been a problem so far. For the first three days Liesel had been with me, and we did everything you do on your first visit to Jerusalem. For openers we went to the top of the YMCA and looked down at the city. It was twilight, and the lovely stone and marble buildings that rose out of the Judean Hills as though they had been planted there like trees or bushes, glowed with a purplish light that slowly faded into a dark pink. We wandered the narrow streets of the old city together, pausing in the narrow alleyways of the market to finger rugs which dangled from canvas booths and to sift chains of ancient gold and strings of beads through our cupped hands. Liesel bought a beautiful striped caftan, and I bought a huge copper tray for my grandfather and twin jackets made of sheepskin for my parents. They smelled terrible, but the merchant swore to me on the life of his father, his children, his wife, my father, and my grandfather that the cleaner would get the smell out. I believed him although, as I told Liesel, I couldn't see that he incurred much risk by swearing on the lives of *my* relatives. Still, I thought my mother and father would look cute traipsing through Central Park in their matching jackets, and it occurred to me that it was silly to think of your parents as looking "cute." That was the way parents were supposed to think about children. Well, I guess that in my family, roles got a little reversed, as the psychologist who came to Chatham every one in a while to discuss "human relations" used to say. Aha, an insight, I said to myself and decided to buy myself a jacket, too. Why should I be the only one in the family who didn't match?

Liesel and I went to the western wall of the temple and I watched Jews with long beards, dressed in the black coats and fur hats of a ghetto that had vanished a hundred years ago, pray side by side with young soldiers and businessmen. I moved very close so that I could touch the ancient stones which were smooth as silk to my fingers. An old woman standing next to me bent to kiss the stone, and I wondered if it had been worn smooth by the lips and prayers of those who visited it.

We went to the Dome of the Rock and stood quietly in the nave of the Church of the Holy Sepulchre as a young monk circled the room, lighting the slender tapers.

The third morning we went to Yad VaShem, walking there from our hostel. I had thought of going, but it was Liesel who suggested it; and although I felt uneasy about going with her I knew Liesel too well to try to argue her out of it. Yad VaShem is a memorial to the six million Jews who were killed by the Germans in World War II. It was Liesel (whose Hebrew was much better than mine) who explained to me that the Hebrew words mean "hand and name" and are from a quotation in the Book of Isaiah where the prophet says that God will give to everyone ". . . in mine house and within my temple walls a place and . . . an everlasting name that shall not be cut off." I thought it was a beautiful idea—that every single life counted forever and was remembered from generation to generation. We walked up to the memorial through the Avenue of the Righteous Gentiles where all the slender trees and saplings were planted as an ever green symbol of gratitude to those who tried to help the Jews during those terrible times. Liesel read the names very carefully, and she stood for several minutes in front of one young tree planted to honor a Hamburg family who, at risk to their own lives, had hidden four Jewish boys. One bough of the tree had withered, and she plucked it off gently.

"We have family in Hamburg," she said, and I didn't answer because there really wasn't anything to say.

We walked up a broad stairway to the memorial shrine which is built of marvelously smooth boulders carried down from the mountains of the Galilee, and then went through great metal gates into a dim hall, its sunken floor tiled with gray black mosaics. There, a cone of sunlight filtered through the tentlike roof and lit up the eternal flame which burned above a casket of human ashes from the ovens of the crematoria. We looked down onto twenty-two ceramic floor panels, each engraved with the name of a concentration camp—Auschwitz, Bergen-Belsen, Buchenwald, Dachau, Theresienstadt. . . .

I thought that there must be some prayer that I should say, but no words came, although I saw that Liesel's lips were moving and tears stood in her bright blue eyes.

Oh God, I thought, please, don't ever let anything like this happen again. I said that over and over again to myself.

Liesel and I went inside and moved slowly through the photographic display. We saw the scenes of Jewish life in Europe as it had once been and then the rise of anti-Semitism—the symbols of hatred. We stood for a long time in front of the picture of a small boy in an oversized winter coat. He had a too-large cap perched on his head, and his hands were raised in surrender, his eyes wide with terror and despair. Liesel began sobbing, her fists clenched, her shoulders shaking.

"Liesel, stop. It has nothing to do with you. You weren't there. You didn't do anything."

But I was crying, too, and I hadn't been there and I had not suffered.

"But someone must be responsible," she murmured.

She spoke in German, and the woman who worked at the information desk turned and looked at her and then swiftly went back to her work, her mouth set, her eyes hard. Understanding takes a long time, forgiveness even longer, I thought and took Liesel's hand in my own.

We walked back across the Avenue of the Righteous Gentiles.

"If you had lived then, Liesel," I said, "there would be a tree here for you."

"But I live now; so I must do my work now," she replied.

She left Jerusalem that night to return to Sadot HaEmek, and I knew without her telling me, that she would volunteer to work double shift during the Chanukah holiday and that the desperate eyes of the small boy who had died so many years ago on a Warsaw street would be in her mind as she worked.

Poor Liesel, I thought, and I felt sorry then for everyone caught up in a net of history that was not of their weaving; for Nimra, caught between her father's ancient quarrels and customs and her yearning for a new life; for Rina and Yaakov, who moved through the shadow of prejudices; for Udi, crippled in a war that had not brought peace. And, of course, I managed to summon up a couple of scraps of self-pity for Lori Mandell.

That was why I was on a street corner in the center of Jerusalem that cold night. I hadn't wanted to hang around the hostel where I really didn't know anyone and which was full of American and English kids who kept practicing idiomatic expressions, telling each other that "this dessert finds favor in my eyes" or that the pimply faced Southern African boy who had just celebrated his eighteenth birthday was "increasing in days." I'd decided to solve my loneliness and the blue mood I was rapidly sinking into by drowning myself in a movie—a time-honored remedy that had never failed before. But when I got to town I discovered that although there were six movie houses, three of them were showing the same film (which I had seen), that I had already seen two of the others in New York, and that the last possibility was a monster movie, and I just didn't feel desperate enough for that. Clutching my potato, I wandered down the hill to Jaffa Road and saw the lights of the Cafe Alaska. I decided to have a hot coffee topped with whipped cream and then head back to the hostel.

I shoved open the door and allowed the warmth of the bright room to wash over me. The small, colorful formica tables were crowded, and the radio blared an interview between the Prime Minister and a new immigrant from Russia; no one was listening. A group of kids sat at a corner table, their backs to me, clustered around a guy who was playing a guitar that was badly out of tune. Two waitresses darted around, depositing plates of cream-covered pastry and scooping up empty coffee cups. The phone rang and the cashier, who stood behind the copper espresso machine, yelled out a name.

"Goldstein, telephone!"

The moustachioed little man who had been reading a gossip magazine glanced at his watch and jumped up to take his call, and I quickly claimed his seat. But before I could order, the kids who had been listening to the guitarist got up to go, and standing there in the red parka I'd helped her pick out at Lord & Taylor was my best friend, Marcie Edel.

"Marcie!"

"Lori!"

We shrieked wildly at each other, then hugged and yelled again.

Everyone turned around to look at us, but since everyone in Israel stares at everyone else anyway, I really didn't care. Our arms entwined, we managed to edge our way out of the cafe through the narrow doorway and onto Jaffa Road.

"I called Balfouria when we got to Jerusalem this afternoon and they said you were here. Then

I tried the number they gave me, and they said you were in the city. Wow! What luck."

Marcie introduced me to the kids she was with—one or two I had known at Chatham. We decided to go back to the hotel they were staying at on King George Street.

Marcie talked a blue streak as we walked there, catching me up on Chatham gossip. Kenny was in Spain with his Spanish class, and a group of kids who were taking anthropology were in South America. I didn't tell her about my "excellent" in physics; it seemed a little pale next to excursions to the Andes. Kenny had a new girl whose claim to fame was the fact that she was only sixteen years old and had lived in sixteen different cities—her father's climb on the corporate ladder sent the family scurrying back and forth across country. I guessed that was why Kenny had never answered my letters, and I wondered why I didn't feel anything at all. After all, we had gone together, sort of. I told Marcie about the friends I had made at Balfouria and at Sadot HaEmek and a little bit about Nimra. I kept waiting for her to ask me questions, but she didn't seem too interested in anything I said. When I talked about the music notebook I was keeping, she let out a yawn.

"You're not getting to be a grind, are you, Lori?" she asked and poked me in the arm.

"No, of course not," I said.

When Marcie asked me about guys I just mumbled something about how there really wasn't much time for dating. I knew for sure that I didn't want to talk to her about Danni.

We all packed into one room at the Kings Hotel and piled our coats and sweaters on the bed. It was the first time I'd been in a centrally heated room since the Thanksgiving dinner at the ZOA House, and it felt good to be warm again and even better to be talking English. I hadn't realized what a strain it was to hesitate over every word in Hebrew or to talk the careful, simple English that Rina and my other Israeli friends understood.

The guitarist tuned up and sang "Blowing in the Wind." Then I took the guitar from him and strummed songs I hadn't played for a long time, like "Wandering Boy" and "You Read it in the *Daily News*." One of the girls lit up a joint and the heavy, sweet odor of grass filled the room. Marcie called room service and a waiter came up with a tray full of cokes. Someone found a cellophane bag of Bachman pretzels and I almost cried. Imagine munching a Bachman pretzel in the heart of Jerusalem. I almost felt that I was home again, but when they passed the joint to me I shook my head and was glad Marcie was busy opening cokes and didn't notice.

"Where's the teacher who's supposed to be traveling with you?" I asked.

"Mr. Connally? He's having dinner with the rabbi, the priest, and the Muslim elder who are going to lead the seminar tomorrow. An ecumenical feast," Marcie said. "He'll be back by eleven, I guess. It'll give us time to get rid of the joints and air the room."

I glanced down at my watch. It was ten-fifteen and the bus left at ten-thirty. If I ran I could just make it to the bus stop and be back at the hostel before they locked up. I scrambled into my layers of sweaters and my coat.

"Say, don't have a heart attack. If you don't make the bus you can sleep here. Connally won't even notice it. He's in a mystical trance half the time," Marcie said.

"You don't understand. I promised I'd be back in time," I said. The one person in the world I didn't want to disappoint was Avraham Macovi because somehow, when I disappointed the old man, I disappointed myself too.

I ran all the way back to the bus stop in the center of town, but just as I got there I saw the yellow glow of its headlights as the bus pulled away. I had missed it by about a minute. I stood there soaking with perspiration that made me shiver beneath my layers of clothing, and panting with exhaustion. The tears that I hadn't shed that afternoon when Liesel left threatened to overflow now. Why was I always screwing everything up? It always had to be me that got caught. I felt the familiar chorus of "Poor Lori" begin to stir within me. Stop that, I said sharply to myself and leaned against the bus stop.

"Lori!" A familiar voice pierced the quiet street. I searched the darkness and saw a car parked there.

A young man got out of the car and walked toward me and I moved back. I didn't know him. I could see the headlines now. American Girl Becomes Jerusalem's First Mugging Victim. But muggers didn't grin widely at you and put out their hands.

"Shalom," the stranger said. "I am Amnon, Udi Eron's friend. Udi is in the car waiting for you."

I followed him back to the car, and sure enough, there was Udi, smiling at me half shyly, half slyly.

"I thought I'd keep an eye on you," he said. "They told me at the hostel you had gone into the city, and I wanted to be sure you caught the last bus. Well, I guess you didn't. Come on, Amnon here will drive you back."

Gratefully, I climbed into the little Fiat, and I was grateful, too, that Amnon and Udi didn't talk. It was funny. Udi had worried secretly about my wandering about alone in Jerusalem just the way I worried secretly about him and what was happening between him and Pnina.

When the car stopped in front of the hostel, I reached out and touched him on the shoulder.

"Good night, Udi. And thank you. Thank you, Amnon."

"It was nothing. Good night, Lori."

I watched the lights of the little car disappear down the hill into the darkness and I heard the wind sing as it wafted through the gently swaying cypress trees. Below me the lights of Jerusalem glistened like small diamonds in a wonderful tiara.

CHAPTER ELEVEN

"Did you have a good time?" Danni asked.

It was our last night in Jerusalem. Chanukah was over and so was Danni's leave and my vacation. We had spent that last evening at a concert at the Hebrew University and we made our way back to the center of the city across the Valley of the Cross. The crisp night air smelled of the clean cold of the season, and the leaves of the ancient olive trees glowed like silver tapers in the velvety darkness. Danni's hand was comforting on my shoulder, and once we stopped in a clearing and looked across the valley at the monastery. As we stood there, the glowing golden lights in the arched windows slowly disappeared, one by one, and the building was left in darkness except for a blaze of candlelight through the arch-shaped windows of the refectory.

"I had a wonderful time," I said and rested my head against him. He bent toward me, and I could feel his breath warm against my neck.

"Sweet Lori," he said and kissed me.

Above us the stars stood still like frozen fragments of silver, and a sudden wind moaned its way through the valley, ruffling Danni's hair and whipping my scarf. Then hand in hand we started downhill and walked back to the city that stretched before us.

It had been a marvelous week. Danni had arrived early—two days after I'd bumped into Marcie and the kids from Chatham. We had all gone together to Chanukah candlelighting ceremonies at the temple wall, and each night for the eight nights of Chanukah, we found ourselves listening to the prayers and blessings, as one candle was added to another, in a different situation. One night we had gone with the kids from Chatham to a *latke* and candlelighting party at the Hillel House in Rehavia, and the next night we joined Udi and his roommate Amnon in their small apartment, one of several which the government had designed for disabled veterans. As Pnina had told us, Udi was getting around on crutches, and he talked excitedly about new hand canes which had been designed so that he would be able to maneuver himself even more easily. He was even learning to drive a special car with hand controls.

"The next time you miss a bus, Lori, I won't have to rely on Amnon to drive you back. I'll do it myself," he said jokingly, but this time there wasn't even the hint of malice in his laughter.

When he carried the coffee to the table I saw that he was easily as tall as Danni, and when his face was relaxed, he was as handsome as his father. I noticed then for the first time his cleft chin that would give Kirk Douglas competition. That night, was a beginning. We spoke to each other, rather than at each other.

But what really surprised me was that Marcie, who had thought Danni a mild "cute" decided that Udi was really sensational. She met him when he joined us for a candlelighting ceremony at the Kings Hotel, and they spent the entire evening in a corner talking; that is, Udi talked and Marcie gasped and said "oh" or "ah" or made other brilliant contributions which didn't seem to dampen Udi's flow. She saw him again a couple of times before her group left Jerusalem, and I saw her address tacked up on the bulletin board on his kitchen wall; so I guess that she had graduated from the "ohs" and "ahs" into at least a promise of letters. I wondered what Pnina would think of that, and then I remembered Ezer and decided that it was none of Pnina's business. It was all very confusing, and as I saw it, Udi's romantic life had moved from a triangle (Udi, Pnina, and Ezer) to a square (Udi, Pnina, Ezer, and Marcie). It wasn't till months later that I found out that the only confusion existed in my own mind.

Danni and I went to Jericho which is supposed

to be the oldest city in the world and certainly looks it. We had lunch at one of the old hotels and Danni told me that Jericho, because of its warmer climate, had once been a big resort area.

"But its real future, I think," he said, "lies in agriculture. They have more water here than anywhere in the area. What could be done for their orange and clementina crops! Perhaps when I finish at the agricultural school I could work at the field station here—experiment with rotating crops."

"It must be wonderful," I said, "to really know what you want to do with your life—the way you and Udi and Rina and Nimra do."

I always thought in terms of next week or next month—or maybe in a really long-term streak of next year and getting into college. But Udi thought of completing his doctorate, Nimra (in more optimistic moments) of getting her degree in agriculture, and Rina was committed to pioneering a new settlement.

"Do you ever think of what you want to do?" Danni asked softly.

"Well, I love working in the greenhouses," I said, "but I'm not much interested in really studying botany. I think what I really like is being alone—listening to my thoughts the way I listen to the plants growing and breathing."

"I know," Danni said. "My best times, too, were in the greenhouses." His fingers reached out and twisted their way through my own so that our two hands together lay on the table in the pale, winter sunshine like a large flower, its petals entwined and closed.

"And I'm good in physics, but I don't ever really feel involved in it," I was thinking aloud now, making up a list of my aptitudes.

"And then there's my music," I said and was quiet because, as though on cue, two small Arab boys began piping a tune on reed flutes. They circled the restaurant, holding out a battered tambourine into which the guests threw coins.

"Yes, that is very important," Danni said and put a folded pound note into the tambourine as the boys passed us. I was glad that he had, because neither of the kids was wearing shoes.

I poured myself some more coffee from the copper pot which the harried waiter had left on the table and thought about my music. I'd always played an instrument—the piano, the flute, and then the guitar—but they had always seemed like toys to me; but then, everything was a toy and every activity a game. It was only since I'd been in Israel and started collecting the various melodies that I began to take the music seriously. Or maybe it was that it was only now that I was taking myself seriously because other people seemed to. That would take some figuring out. Meanwhile I nodded at Danni.

"Yes, I think my music is important," I agreed, and I was surprised at using the word "important." Could I, Lori Mandell, really be hooked on something important? Maybe. On that afternoon in Jericho, as the sun turned Danni's hair the color of honey and we left the restaurant to walk together through the maze of narrow cobble-stoned lanes, I felt that anything was possible in the best of all possible worlds.

But now the Chanukah week was over. Marcie and her group had already left Jerusalem to go skin diving in Elath—very relevant to a course in Judeo-Christian tradition; but having met their teacher Mr. Connally, I knew he'd find a way to justify it. I'd felt bad saying goodbye to Marcie. She was a part of me—a part of the life I'd always known even though we were both pretty embar-rassed when we hugged goodbye to find out that we were both crying. We'd never done that be-fore.

"It must be the altitude," Marcie said, dabbing at her eyes with a Kleenex. "Anyway, you'll be home in a couple of months, Lori. And hey—re-mind Udi to write to me. Or do you think I should write to him first?"

And then she was off, leaving me her Levi jacket, a pair of bib overalls, and half a bottle of Breck for oily hair.

I was wearing the bib overalls on that last night in Jerusalem, and as we sat in the lounge of the hostel, Danni played with the denim straps. I loved the feel of his fingers through the fabric of my blouse and when I sat tall next to him the stubble of his beard scraped my chin and I liked that feeling too. But that didn't stop me from feeling as though the world was coming to an end. I felt tears beginning to form and I hoped that Danni would leave before I began to cry.

"Lori, don't cry." His voice was soft because there were other kids in the lounge, most of them talking very loudly to show that they were having a really terrific time.

"I'm not crying," I said, which became a lie at that moment when the tears began to pour down my face. The thing was I didn't even know why I felt so miserable. It had been a great week, and Danni would have another leave soon.

"When I was a small boy I always cried after my birthday parties—just because they had been so wonderful. And you know, when I go to a special concert and it is over, I cry sometimes because it was so beautiful. I felt like crying after the concert tonight." His voice soothed me, the way my grandfather's used to when I was a small girl crying over something that couldn't be helped.

"I don't mind that you are crying, because it was such a wonderful week for us," he said.

"Oh Danni!" I put my arms around him, and it didn't matter at all that the room was crowded and a phone was ringing.

We walked to the door together, and he kissed me hard on the mouth, then lightly on the forehead, his hand cupping my chin. I watched him walk down the path and I didn't feel like crying anymore. I felt warm all the way through; a smile seemed to have pasted itself across my face and I wasn't about to peel it off; my skin glowed and when I passed a mirror I saw that my eyes kind of glittered. Now I knew what people meant when they said they were happy. I, Lori Mandell, in the city of Jerusalem in December of 1976 was a happy girl, and no matter what happened, no one could ever take that away from me. I looked out the window and waved jauntily to the stars that trembled toward me through the thick darkness of a night I would always remember.

CHAPTER TWELVE

The weeks after Chanukah went slowly at first, and then suddenly they began to tumble by. An entire semester was over, and I knew I'd made a good beginning when the teacher in my spring semester social studies class, who hadn't been told I was a visiting American, asked me a question in Hebrew and I actually answered it. Of course my grammar was all screwed up and a couple of the kids laughed, but it was a happy kind of laughter. My parents began calling regularly once a week and they were interested in what I was doing; always before it had seemed to me that all they wanted was for me to reassure them that I was having a good time or that if I wasn't, that I really didn't care. Now they truly wanted to know. It was as though I had to go away for them to realize that I wasn't there. I told my mother about the music collection that I was making, and the next thing I knew, a publisher friend of hers wrote me a letter asking if she could see my note book. I copied out what I had, with some of the explanations, and sent it to her. I didn't really expect anything to happen, but it was a good feeling to know that someone was interested in what I was doing.

Shalom-Salaam outgrew his stall, and Avraham Macovi built a wider enclosure for him.

"Now he has room," he said with satisfaction when he was finished. "Animals are like people. They need room to grow."

Shalom-Salaam moaned happily in agreement and spit some hay at us. His large, dark eyes roamed the barn and he stretched lazily.

"But even this stall will not be good for him for much longer. He is not an animal of the barnyard. Soon a new time will come in his life, Lori," the old man continued.

"No!" I said too loudly.

I didn't want a new time to come. I wanted things to stay as they were, with the air growing warmer and sweeter, with Rina and myself sharing our lives as though we were sisters, and Danni's letters making my fingers tingle and my heart beat faster.

I wouldn't have minded having a little more time though. During those months everyone at Balfouria was working at a frenetic pace. Gad's father, who was what I guess you could call a resident botanist, had developed an iris so delicate and lovely that people were calling it the Balfouria Orchid. It was the pale lavender color of the drifting clouds of the Galilean sky after a swift and sudden rainfall; its soft petals stretched outward and then came together barely showing the deep purple threads of the pistil. The Balfouria cooperative had been flooded with orders from Europe, and every family was working around the clock at the greenhouses to meet the contracts. For weeks Esther and Chaim Eron had been waking at five o'clock in the morning and working into the evening. Rina and I helped them when we came home from school, and our fingers were stained green by the stems of the fragile flowers that bled as we shifted them to catch the sunlight that beamed down from a network of ultra-violet lamps. The success of the Balfouria Orchid would make a big difference to Balfouria. The collective could build its own school, raise the incomes of its members, expand the library. I knew that Esther and Chaim Eron had not had a vacation for ten years.

"They save everything so that we can go to university," Rina said. "But now with these orders, all that will change. There will be money for everything."

During the last week in March we worked feverishly, crating the flowers, packing them in dry ice for their trip across the Mediterranean. A special cargo vessel had been chartered, and on a pale morning, when clouds that matched our flower hovered over us, we loaded the trucks and watched them drive off on their way to Haifa port. Chaim Eron and the other drives wore small iris buds in the buttonholes of their work shirts and Esther Eron had stuck a flower through her long, dark hair. The women sang as the trucks pulled away, and a group of children dashed after them, scattering handfuls of wild flowers that had only just begun to poke their way upward on the hillsides. Rina picked up a cluster of blood-red anemones and threaded them through her hair.

"I love these flowers," she said, "and so does Yaakov."

She was still wearing them when Esther came up to our room that afternoon to tell Rina she had a guest. I knew from her voice, which mingled reserve and surprise, that there was something special about this guest and I wasn't really surprised, minutes later, to hear Rina's happy scream and Yaakov's deep, gentle voice.

I gave her fifteen minutes and then followed Rina downstairs. She and Yaakov were in the kitchen drinking tall glasses of grapefruit juice, placing the glasses so close to each other on the table that their fingers touched as they lifted them. They were staring at each other, and as I stood there, Yaakov reached up, took a tiny anemone from Rina's hair and tucked it into the insignia on his uniform. I hadn't seen Yaakov in uniform before and I had to admit that he looked even better than Danni. Danni's uniforms were always rumpled and creased, but Yaakov's olive green trousers and shirt were as crisp as the curtains in his mother's small kitchen, and his red beret was carefully brushed. His dark skin glowed with a desert sheen. I noticed for the first time the glints of amber in his eyes.

"Hi, Yaakov." I tossed him the brisk salute Danni had taught me, and he laughed and returned it.

"Lori. Always the joke. It is good to see you. I am on my way to a camp on the border and the road goes right by Balfouria. I thought I would surprise Rina."

"Yeah, sure, terrific," I said, thinking that Rina wasn't the only one who would be surprised.

Esther Eron came in then, her arms full of sheets which she had plucked from the line.

"Can you stay for the night, Yaakov?" she asked politely, but I saw a wave of relief cross her face when he refused.

"No. I must be at the camp by five. There is an alert out for infiltrators. But I thank you very much for the invitation."

Esther nodded.

"Next time perhaps." She threw Rina a sharp glance, but I saw that it was a glance of concern rather than disapproval. Esther was the calming force in the household. She had learned the art of mediation from her father, Avraham Macovi. Gently, patiently, she tried to bridge the gap between her *sabra* children and her husband whose childhood and youth had been lived in the black terror of the concentration camps. Sometimes in the night I heard her talk softly to Rina or to Danni or Udi, after a harsh discussion.

"You must understand your father. He had a hard life. It has left him frightened."

And then, too, I heard her talk to her husband, her voice soothing.

"Chaim, you must change your ideas. This is a new country with new things happening. Didn't we fight for a land for all Jews? Then we must welcome all Jews, respect them, learn from them."

But as far as I could see, she had done little to change Chaim Eron's negative feelings about those Jews whom he called, with quiet anger, "the black ones." "They" demanded too much of the country which he had helped to reclaim and build at the risk of his own life. "They," with their constant demands and enormous families that drained the welfare resources of the state. "They," who complained constantly about their bad housing. Had "they" lived in tents mired in swamps as Avraham Macovi's family had? Had "they" reached the country in a battered Greek vessel that held three hundred refugees although it was built to transport perhaps a hundred passengers? Had "they" swum to shore in the dead of night with the bullets of British soldiers ringing above their heads through the darkness? No. "They" had been flown in, in air-conditioned El Al planes, and yet "they" complained and called for strikes and sit-ins.

Rina, Udi, Danni, and lately, when I had the nerve, even I, argued with him. Maybe, Udi had suggested wryly, we should recreate the Huleh swamp so that the recent immigrants could have a chance to get malaria and prove that they were sacrificing for the Jewish state. Danni pointed out that his father grimaced when he drove past the slums of Tel Aviv; so why did he object to people demanding improved housing? Certainly "they" had done their share in the defense forces. Some of the best officers he had served under and his closest friends in the army had been those Jews his father dismissed as "the black ones." And Rina, who seldom argued with anyone, asked her father if it weren't true that Israelis were encouraged to have large families, that population was important to the young country.

"And don't we need Jews to replace those killed in the camps?" she had asked. Chaim Eron's nostrils flared in anger, and his eyes burned with a fierce sorrow they did not understand. He slammed out of the room. Clearly, she had gone too far, and it was Esther who hurried after him, her face troubled. Through the window they saw her catch up with him and slowly walk with him to the citron orchard, her arm around her husband's shoulder as though he were a small boy whom she was comforting after a terrible loss, a secret sorrow. The young people sat alone in the kitchen talking softly. I had gone to the barn to check on Shalom-Salaam.

"What's it all about? Who's right? Who's wrong?" I asked my little camel who looked at me with his huge mournful eyes, the lashes standing straight up. He brayed gently—about as good an answer as I could hope to get.

"Rina, why don't you and Lori show Yaakov around Balfouria?" Esther suggested.

I started to protest, thinking that Rina and Yaakov needed me the way Danni's Vespa needed a third wheel, but I caught the look in Esther's eyes. She wanted us all out so that she could prepare Chaim for Yaakov's arrival. I flashed a signal back at her and went with my friends, figuring that we would soon find a way to lose each other.

It was a perfect day to be showing off Balfouria. We stopped at the Eron greenhouse, and I showed Yaakov our famous orchid. He was impressed but disappointed because its fragrance was so light.

"You know they are doing wonderful work with flowers in some Negev kibbutzim. You know so much about it, Rina. When we start our kibbutz perhaps that could be one of our projects. It would be so much better to raise flowers than to make spare parts for television sets as they do at Sadot HaEmek."

"Why not?" Rina said, holding her hands out in the typical Israeli gesture of agreement.

I decided that they really had progressed since last summer at Sadot HaEmek. Now Yaakov said "when" not "if." I guess Rina must have been describing more than snow in those ten-page letters.

When we had exhausted the recreation room,

the library, and the synagogue and there was still no sign of the Balfouria trucks returning from Haifa, I suggested that we borrow a car and ride over to the Nashifs and introduce Yaakov to Nimra. I thought that Nimra, who had taken the examination for the university weeks before, might have had the results. Although I was certain that she had passed, I wanted to hear it from her. By the time we would get back Chaim Eron would have arrived, and Esther would have had time to prepare him for Yaakov.

The windows of the Nashif house were covered by heavy, black draperies and the door was tightly closed. For a moment I thought that they were not at home, but then I saw two of the smaller children playing at the side of the house. They were drawing in the dry soil with a curved olive branch. I saw Hulda moving among the trees, breaking off branches that had grown too brittle during the winter. When she saw us it seemed to me that she began hurrying at her work, although she did not immediately move toward us. The children shouted something and the black curtain moved, revealing a chevron of window. Through it, I saw Nimra's face peer out anxiously, and seconds later, she opened the door.

"Lori, Rina. How good to see you," she said.

Rina introduced her to Yaakov, and Nimra smiled her shy, gentle smile.

"Do you mind if I show Yaakov the orchard?" Rina asked and Nimra nodded. I watched them walk together across the ground that was dappled with the star-shaped shadows of the silvery olive leaves, their hands locked as though they would never let each other go. I wondered where Danni was just then, thinking that that was the way we had walked together, that last night in Jerusalem, through the Valley of the Cross.

Nimra jolted me back to the present.

"Lori, I have heard from the university. I passed the examination and I may enroll. They offer me the scholarship Avraham Macovi spoke of."

"That's wonderful!" I hugged her and was startled when she stood passively by. "What's the matter, Nimra?"

"The passing doesn't make any difference," she said bitterly, and I saw that her dark eyes were awash with tears. "My father will not let me go."

"But Avraham Macovi will talk to him. Surely he will change his mind."

"No. Nothing will change his mind. I must go in now. Tell Rina and her friend shalom."

Again, I saw the black window drape move, and then Nimra slipped inside and I heard the low murmur of voices. I watched the children break the olive branch into a neat pile of sticks and improvise a game of pick-up-sticks. Games remained the same all over the world, I thought. Why did people have to be so different? I waited in a patch of shade until Rina and Yaakov returned, their faces bright with the pure joy of being with each other.

We sang as we drove back to Balfouria, and

Yaakov taught us a new song that he had learned in the army.

"Do you like the army?" I asked him.

"I don't dislike it," he said, and I thought that he and Chaim Eron were definitely on the same conversational wavelength.

Esther was waiting for us on the porch. She had prepared an afternoon snack which was laid out on the kitchen table, and we settled down hungrily to the cheeses, herring in wine sauce, salads, and enormous cups of coffee. Esther, who had already eaten, smiled at our appetites and went back outside, leaving the screen door open. The trucks were very late in returning, and it occurred to me that now she was eager for Yaakov to be gone before Chaim came back. Twice she had reminded him that he still had many miles to go before reaching his border assignment.

We chatted easily as we ate. Yaakov told us that Liesel was working in the children's house now and that his sister Yaffa followed her everywhere. I was briefly jealous and then I thought of my tall, blond friend walking hand in hand with the tiny black girl whose eyes danced with mischief, and I smiled at the mental picture. There were plans to take all the children of Sadot HaEmek into Tel Aviv for the *Adloyada*, the big Purim costume parade, and I decided to write Danni and see if he could arrange leave for that day.

Then, during a brief lull in our talk, I heard

footsteps outside and Chaim Eron's deep voice, riddled with anger.

"You are surprised that we are late? You will be more surprised to hear what has happened. Our trucks missed the cargo ship. We were held up for four hours on the road by a strike. For four hours we could not move while the road workers made their point. Those lazy *shechorim*—those good-for-nothing black ones. If they don't like it here let them go back to the countries they came from. Who needs them? When there is no school at Bal-fouria because we have lost the profit from the or-chid, think of your black friends."

We heard Esther's soft voice, but we sat in frozen silence, as though Chaim's words of hatred had paralyzed us. Rina put her hand over Yaakov's slender black fingers, the half moons of his nails pale because he was clenching the table as a child sometimes grasps something solid to keep from crying. He pulled away and rose slowly.

"Yaakov, please," Rina said, her voice breaking. "He was upset, disappointed. He did not mean it."

"Of course he meant it," Yaakov said in a dull tone. "This is why I have not been asked here be-fore, Rina. You should have been honest."

"Yaakov, please." She was crying now, and he moved toward her but stopped. Chaim Eron had come into the room. He stood uncertainly in the doorway, his sharp, blue eyes darting from his weeping daughter to the young black-skinned soldier. It was Yaakov Gamliel who moved first. He shouldered his gun and without turning around, left the house through the kitchen door, closing it very softly behind him.

"Yaakov!" Rina screamed and ran to the window.

He turned then and their eyes met for a long minute. Pain and anger filled the silence that stretched between them. He waved at last and walked on. Rina watched him until his slight form disappeared over a gentle hillside. With tears streaming down her cheeks, she ran upstairs, hurtling past her father who stood unmoving in the doorway.

CHAPTER THIRTEEN

Purim day brought the first real warmth of spring, and as we dressed that morning Rina and I saw a family of storks swoop through the lime green sky on their way southward to the swales of Lake Tiberias. Rina smiled briefly, but her eyes retained the veil of heavy misery that had clouded them since Yaakov's visit. She had written twice, but he had not answered. We knew, because Pnina had written to Udi that Yaakov was still on the northern border, and when the hourly news came on, Rina remained very still, assuming the pose of all the women of Israel whose men patrol uneasy borders.

"Maybe Yaakov will be at the *Adloyada* with the group from Sadot HaEmek," I said.

"No, I don't think so," Rina said sadly, but I noticed that she wore a gold blouse that picked up the flecks of gold in her dark eyes and that she brushed her long hair into silken folds about her shoulders instead of weaving it into a schoolgirl braid.

There was little conversation at breakfast. There had, in fact, been little conversation at any of the meals the Eron family had shared since that day. Rina was icily polite to her father, and both of them ignored any attempts made by Avraham Macovi, Esther, or myself to break the angry silence between them.

"You should try to understand your father," I said to Rina one night after we had finished our homework and were getting ready for bed.

"Why?" she asked bitterly. "Have you ever tried to understand your parents? All you've done since you've been here is complain about them; you say they're frivolous, they're selfish, that they think only about themselves. But they've never tried to control your life the way my father would control mine. And your mother works for civil rights—she doesn't deny people's equality the way my father does. You know, Lori, in spite of everything you told me, I like your parents. The problem is, I'm not sure I like my father."

She turned away from me then and I knew she was crying. I lay awake for a long time that night thinking about what she had said. She was right, I knew. During those long hours, when the silence of the Galilean night was broken only by the distant shriek of a mountain jackal, I thought about my parents, about their terrific energy, the way they grabbed at life; I liked them too, I decided, and I was smiling when at last I fell asleep.

We drove into Tel Aviv with Udi who had spent several days at Balfouria. He was driving now—a special car with hand controls—and he was proud of the bright red auto and the way he handled it. Although sometimes the old familiar bitterness thinned his lips and dulled his eyes, and his remarks could still be pretty sarcastic, he was a different Udi from the young man in the wheelchair whom I had met my first day at Balfouria.

The Haifa Road was crowded. The country was in a holiday mood, and motorists shouted good-naturedly at each other. Costumed children in caravans of buses gaily sang Purim songs in praise of the brave and beautiful queen Esther who had, long ago, saved the Jews of Persia, and they hissed when they came to the name of Haman, the evil villain who had threatened to destroy them. There were children in open trucks who playfully tapped each other on the head with the light, plastic hammers they called "patiches." The very young children carried Purim noisemakers, and when we stopped for a red light, the road hummed with their urgent whirling and rattling. Queen Esther had been pretty smart to schedule her life-saving act at the beginning of spring.

The streets of Tel Aviv were clogged with cars, but Udi found a parking space in a special area that had been reserved for disabled drivers.

"See," he said. "This is a fringe benefit of the Yom Kippur War."

With Udi balancing on his hand crutches, we slowly made our way to the corner where we had agreed to meet our friends from Sadot HaEmek. All the children were there, and Yaffa darted away from Liesel to plant a wet kiss on my cheek and then ran back. Liesel and I hugged, and I realized that I hadn't seen her since our visit to Yad VaShem. The weeks and months were flying by so quickly, and there never seemed to be enough time. Soon, perhaps the next weekend or the one after that, I would go to Sadot HaEmek and spend some time with Liesel, who concentrated now on tying a bright pink ribbon in Yaffa's glossy black hair.

I heard a shriek of "fantasti—exciting" and located Amy and Ellen who were standing arm in arm with Gad and Rafi. Pnina came up to Udi and they wandered off to the edge of the crowd. I saw Rina's eyes swiftly rake over the faces, and her gaze finally met the eyes of Yaakov's mother who smiled sadly and turned away. Gently, I touched Rina's hand.

"She knows what happened," Rina said.

"It wasn't your fault. It was your father who said those things—not you."

"But that doesn't seem to matter to Yaakov or to his parents," she answered. Her voice was very sad.

"Come on. Let's try to forget it and watch the parade," I said, and we turned our attention to the colorful caravan that danced its way down Rothschild Boulevard.

Gaily decorated floats, on which raven-haired Queen Esthers danced nimbly before youthful King Ahasueroses, moved in stately procession. An ensemble of clowns and acrobats tumbled down the street, letting loose bouquets of brightly colored balloons which floated up into the clear, blue sky. Little Yaffa reached up and clutched it triumphantly. Bursts of applause soared skyward and mingled with laughter as a float of marionettes enacting the Purim story in modern dress moved slowly down the avenue. Queen Esther in a mini skirt consulted with her cousin Mordechai, who was grave in horn-rimmed glasses and an "I Love Bach" sweat shirt. The evil Haman wore a motorcycle jacket and tight leather trousers. His slick, dark sideburns matched his cowboy moustache.

"Perhaps I'll grow a moustache like that."

I had been laughing so hard that I hadn't noticed someone sidling up to me. I looked up and fell into Danni's arms.

"I only managed to get an afternoon pass," he said, and then he too began to laugh as the indignant mini-skirted Esther whacked Haman over the head with a paddle. Yaffa jumped happily up and down, her pink balloon and ribbon bobbing in rhythm.

When at last the parade was over, there was not a single unsmiling face in the crowd. Even

Rina had begun to laugh and remained smiling as we wandered off together. Danni, Rina, and I walked arm in arm, and behind us, more slowly, Udi and Pnina strolled. Traffic resumed on the street, and the familiar sounds of busy Tel Aviv filled the air. Horns bleated angrily, brakes screeched, and shouts in a melange of languages filled the air as a farmer in a horse-drawn cart leisurely made his way down the broad avenue, ignoring the furious drivers who shouted at him.

Danni bought Rina and me two yellow patiches, and we giggled and playfully banged each other on the head. Now traffic moved more smoothly, and we stood, still laughing, on a corner and waited for the light to change. I remember looking lazily upward, because I had heard the hum of a helicopter. Soaring across the street was a pink balloon. The next thing I heard was the screech of brakes, a woman's anguished cry, and then a sudden silence enveloped the street which minutes before had been vibrant with noise and gaiety.

"Oh my God," Rina said softly, and I kept my eyes closed because I knew that something terrible had happened.

A woman sobbed wildly and the smell of vomit filled the street as a grown man who had not closed his eyes, heaved noisily. Danni moved quickly forward. Policemen blew their whistles and an ambulance's siren pierced the sudden quiet. Clutching Rina's fingers, I opened my eyes. In the middle of the avenue a body lay, covered with blood and splinters of bone: I saw a familiar blue skirt, covered with blood, and I steeled myself to look at the closed eyes and the almost smiling mouth that had once been my friend Liesel. Next to her, little Yaffa Gamliel wept uncontrollably while her mother cradled her gently and rocked her back and forth.

The doctor looked briefly down at the body and drew a white sheet over the strangely peaceful face. Liesel was dead. Dead. The word echoed strangely through my mind, a frozen group of meaningless letters, and then Rina and I turned to each other and tears streamed down our faces. We were still crying when Danni led us away to a small sidewalk cafe on a nearby street where he told us what had happened. Yaffa's balloon had floated out of her hand and she had dashed after it into the middle of the busy street. A speeding taxi, not noticing the small child, was almost upon her when Liesel dashed forth, pushed Yaffa aside and was herself struck by the car. She had died instantly, Danni told us, and we took some comfort from that.

I thought of the last day I had spent with Liesel, of her anguish at the memories of World War II. I remembered how passionately she had cried out after seeing the photographs of the holocaust that "someone had to be responsible." She had translated those words into action. When Yaffa dashed into the street, Liesel had taken on the responsibility of the child's life. Briefly, I wondered if I would have been capable of saving

Yaffa, but then I stopped thinking about myself and thought of my newly found, newly lost friend, of her long hair the color of cornsilk and of her blue eyes so full of sorrow and gentleness. I thought of all the times we had laughed and talked together and the long walks we had taken at Sadot HaEmek and in Jerusalem. We would never laugh together again. For the very first time I understood the loss and finality of death. Sitting there, with Danni and Rina, in the bright sunlight of the holiday afternoon, I began to cry, and I think, for the first time in my life, my tears were not for myself but for my good, brave friend. We touched hands, as we sat there, the three of us, as though to reassure each other, on that day of death, that we were alive, and we knew now that we must treasure the golden moments of life.

"Poor Liesel," Danni said softly, and I saw that his eyes too were wet. I was proud that he was strong enough to cry.

"Poor good Liesel," Rina added.

We left the cafe then, and it was not until we were in the pickup truck on the way back to Balfouria that I realized that we had left our yellow plastic mallets, the gay Purim patches on the table. But then, toys are for children and on that Purim afternoon we had all crossed one of those frontiers that mark the end of childhood. We had known a friend and lost her. We grieved at her loss and understood her death. We sang softly as we drove northward to Balfouria, songs that talked of passing days and half-remembered nights, of love and friendship, and of morning mists veiling the sea.

"There were times," Gad sang softly, "when we sat and dreamed. Now these times are gone, but in the dream they return."

It was dark when we reached Balfouria, and the first evening stars hung above us like silvery teardrops.

CHAPTER FOURTEEN

Liesel's body was flown back to Germany for burial, but a service was held for her in Israel as well. Sadot HaEmek planted a cypress tree in her memory. We drove there for the ceremony with Rafi and Gad and watched as little Yaffa Gamliel tenderly placed the slender sapling in the ground and carefully packed the soft earth about its network of fragile roots. I thought of the day when Liesel and I had walked beneath the trees that lined the Avenue of the Righteous Gentiles on Mount Herzl and how the leaves of those memorial trees had cast star-shaped shadows through her fair hair. Pnina talked about Liesel then, of her goodness and gentleness, and above all her sense of responsibility.

We were all crying when Pnina finished and we joined hands and sang "*Ani Maamin*," the hymn of the concentration camps. "I believe," we sang. "I believe with perfect faith in the coming of the Messiah." Liesel, too, had believed with perfect faith in the coming of a messianic time when all men would live together in peace.

Yaakov was at the memorial service, and although he did not stand near Rina, they stared at each other, and when the ceremony was over he came toward her and she held her hand out to him. It was the first time that they had seen each other since that terrible afternoon at Balfouria. They walked off together toward the orange groves, and I saw Yaakov stop to pluck a blossom and thread it through Rina's lose, dark hair.

"It will be all right," I said to myself and I went back to the Gamliel house with Yaffa, who was still weepy. We played a game of Monopoly, and by the time Yaffa had three hotels on Boardwalk I was feeling pretty optimistic. I estimated that at the moment of my imminent bankruptcy, Rina and Yaakov would announce their engagement. But just as Yaffa was foreclosing on the last of my mortgages, Yaakov came in alone.

"Rina is waiting for you in the jeep with Gad and Rafi," he said, and his eyes did not meet mine.

I kissed his mother and sisters goodbye and I knew that we wouldn't be hearing wedding bells for a long time.

Rina told me that night that Yaakov had asked her to leave Balfouria and come to live at Sadot

HaEmek. He insisted that if she loved him she would not stay in her father's house.

"What could I say? I told him that I too am miserable because of my father's attitude, but still, I am his daughter. My father has lost everything in his life. His childhood was spent in concentration camps. His parents, his brothers, and sisters, all his family, were killed. We are all he has. Can he lose me now?" Rina held her palms out in bewilderment.

"Perhaps he'll change," I said.

"No, he won't," Rina replied sadly. I thought of Chaim Eron's sharp, blue eyes, the firm set of his chin, the way he clenched and unclenched his fists as though struggling with his own anger. I knew that Rina was right.

But there wasn't much time to brood over things at Balfouria during those weeks. My grandfather called from New York and announced that he was coming to Balfouria for Passover.

"Travel is broadening," he said primly into the phone, which I translated to mean: "Lori, I love you and miss you like crazy."

"Gather ye rosebuds while ye may," I replied and I knew he knew that I meant: "Grandpa, I can hardly wait to see you." It had taken us longer to understand each other's languages than it had taken me to learn workable Hebrew.

Of course Avraham Macovi was delighted and the Erons were pleased, although Esther Eron cast worried looks at her worn slipcovers and re-vamped the menu. Marcie wrote to tell me that my grandfather had called her with a very subtle question like: "If you were spending a year in Is-rael and your grandfather was coming to visit you, what would you want him to bring you?" She also mentioned receiving a couple of letters from Udi and asked if he had received a record that she had sent.

I wrote back to tell her that her heart's desire, if her grandfather were coming, would be a tape re-corder. I did not mention Udi. The tape recorder could be passed on to Danni when I left the coun-try. Then I could always send him cassettes from home in New York. At that point the thought of thousands of miles separating us really hit me, and I left the letter unfinished on my desk and ran out to the barn. I turned for comfort to Shalom-Salaam, who managed to incline his silly neck in such a way that I found a comfortable niche for my head.

"What's going to happen, Shalom-Salaam?" I asked my young camel, and he shifted patiently from one leg to the other and breathed softly into my ear. I always knew that I could expect abso-lute attention and sympathy from him, even if he was not very long on practical advice.

Then, too, we were very busy at school. Rina, who was a year ahead of me, and a lot of the kids we were friendly with, were preparing for the comprehensive examinations which all Israeli kids must take if they want to receive a high school diploma. The test covers everything studied during the four years of high school, and studying for it is a masochistic feat involving endless cups of black coffee, all-night cram sessions, and at least one nervous breakdown in each class. I acted as coach and followed after Rafi, Gad, and Rina throwing out dates, formulas, and irregular verbs. In a way I was glad Rina was studying so hard because it took her mind off Yaakov who hadn't been in touch since the memorial service, although Rina had written him a long, careful letter of explanation.

I concentrated on my own papers and studied for the comprehensive examination in physics, which I had decided to take. I thought it would give Dr. Chalmers something to sit up and think about if irresponsible Lori Mandell (poor undisciplined child) managed to excel in that test. And, of course, we were all busy in the greenhouses trying to make up for the loss of the shipment of the Balfouria orchids that had been delayed. But I did take one weekend off and traveled to Sadot HaEmek to see Yaffa in a play. It was an Israeli version of *Snow White* and my little Ethiopian friend made the cutest princess, even though there were a lot of quiet smiles when the queen's mirror told her that Snow White was "the fairest of them all."

"Darkest maybe, but definitely not fairest," a familiar voice whispered, and I turned my head to see Ezer sitting next to Pnina.

We had coffee together after the performance,

and he offered me a lift to Balfouria. He was traveling north again because there were new signs of terrorist activity on the northern border. Yaakov, too, was stationed there now.

"We cannot understand who is sheltering them," he said worriedly. "They must have a refuge somewhere."

I thought of Nimra's cousin Ibrahim then, but she had told me that her father would no longer welcome him and I believed her. Still, something nagged at me, tugged at my memory, and then I remembered the drawn, dark curtains of the Nashif house. But that didn't mean anything, I assured myself. Lots of people draw their curtains in this country where the harsh sunlight sometimes sears the eyes. Still, I would visit Nimra that week. I had not seen her for a while and I hoped that perhaps her father would have changed his mind. Yes, I would go over to the Nashif house as soon as I returned to Balfouria.

I drove north to Balfouria with Ezer and two of his soldiers. One of them was from Afghanistan, and he taught me a new melody for the song which welcomes the sabbath. I wrote it down in the music notebook that I carried everywhere now. I hadn't heard from the music publisher, but I really didn't care. The important thing was learning the songs and capturing the music. If I ever did publish my notebook, I had decided that I would dedicate it to Liesel.

The days that followed were wildly busy. Esther, Rina, and I concentrated on cleaning the house from top to bottom. Every piece of furniture was carried outside, and we scrubbed floors, cabinets, and walls. The little house smelled sweet and clean—of the new season of green and warmth. Esther began the cooking and we helped prepare mounds of gefilte fish and chopped liver, tureens of chicken soup, pan after pan of roast chicken and duck. The refrigerator was packed full, and Avraham Macovi went to the storage shed and lugged an old ice chest into the house. Together we drove to the Nashifs, and I waited in the jeep while Abdul Nashif and Avraham Macovi piled an enormous chunk of ice wrapped in straw, on the back seat. Nimra was not at home, Abdul told me when I asked. Again I glanced at the house and saw the heavy draperies shielding the window, and again, as I watched, I saw the drape part slightly and a dark eye peer through the chevron of light. But if Avraham Macovi noticed anything, he said nothing. I helped him unload the ice and we settled it into the chest.

"You see," he said, pointing to the legend etched at the bottom of the ancient container, "we brought that chest with us from Germany. For years it was a luxury to us to refrigerate anything at all. We drank our milk warm from the cow's udder and dug underground storage pits for meat and produce. How long ago all that seems when now we use the ice chest for an emergency—for whatever does not fit into the freezer and refrigerator. Ah, yes, those times are past."

But there was a wistfulness in his words as though those bygone days, when Balfouria had been a tent village struggling toward the vanquishing of the swamps, had been simpler, pleasant times. Everyone had worked together then, their dreams focused on a sweet future. There had been no angry, silent quarrels between fathers and daughters; no deep, terrible gulfs between Jews who had come together to reclaim and build a land.

"There were times," the old man sang softly, "when we sat and dreamed." I recognized the song that we had sung as we drove back from Tel Aviv on the night of Liesel's death. How did anyone ever make peace with lost and useless dreams?

A heavy sadness settled on me; the kind of sadness I sometimes felt as I watched a pale twilight drift over the purple mountains. Days were passing so swiftly. Soon I would begin my second summer at Balfouria, and when it was over I would begin packing. Briskly, I brushed the thought aside and hurried in to the warm, bright kitchen which was awash now with the baking odor of sweet sponge and nut cakes, the scent of sugared fruits stewing in an enormous cauldron.

Danni, his paratrooper wings bright on his collar, his uniform pressed to an unusual crispness, Avraham Macovi, spiffed up in a freshly ironed blue shirt, his white hair standing in the usual aureole about his head, and I, in an embroidered white blouse which Yaakov Gamliel's mother had sent me as a gift, and a new navy blue skirt, rode together to Lydda Airport to pick up my grandfather. I wondered what he would think of my new haircut. My long blond hair was gone and my hair had been cut to fit my head like a small gold cap. It was cooler and easier to take care of, and, most important of all, Danni loved it.

The airport was crowded as Israelis ran about trying to locate relatives they had never seen before.

"Uncle Feibish Finkelstein," a tall young man shouted over and over, looking into everyone's face. I was relieved when he located his uncle (a tall old man wearing a Vandyke beard) because he was getting so desperate I was afraid he might even claim me.

A plane of Russian Jews arrived, and I stared as a very old man supported by two young Israelis climbed down the gangplank, reached the ground, and knelt to press his lips against the soil. "*Eretz Yisrael,*" his lips mouthed silently, and a tall soldier standing next to me wiped his eyes without embarrassment.

Crowds of American tourists, clicking their cameras (after all who could return to Schenectady without a snapshot of the Coca-Cola sign in Hebrew?), clambered cheerfully through the waiting room, marveling generously at everything. Jewish porters, Jewish customs agents, Jewish maintenance men. They beamed and distributed bubble gum to every kid in sight.

And then, finally, my grandfather's flight was

announced, and passengers began disembarking, walking with that peculiar jet-lag wobble, looking uncertainly about. But not my grandfather. He clasped his umbrella firmly in one hand, his attaché case (definitely stuffed with countless telex cables, back issues of the *Wall Street Journal* and an assortment of Maalox and gelusil tablets) in the other, and a *Readers' Digest* tucked underneath his arm. He walked staring straight ahead, and as though he were equipped with radar, he headed right for us.

"Grandpa!"

"Lori!"

And then I was in his arms, sniffing the familiar odor of his pine-scented after-shave lotion, my hand on the back of his neck where his short, gray hair grew in spiky tendrils.

Next he embraced Avraham Macovi, and their cheeks were wet with each other's tears. They had been boys together in a town whose streets they could never walk again. They had played together in homes that no longer existed. They had shared the dreams and plans of young men, but they had spent their lives so differently. Still, nothing separated them in this moment of reunion and they wept openly.

Finally, I introduced my grandfather to Danni, whom I had mentioned with casual care in my letters. But nothing deceives a man who makes money on the stock market even in a bad year, and I saw him study Danni swiftly, shrewdly, his eyes taking in the bright, new paratroopers wings and the way Danni stood, so proudly erect, at ease with himself in his land. They shook hands seriously, and somehow I was glad that it was my grandfather who released Danni's hand first.

"Well, how do I look, Grandpa?" I asked, waiting for him to mention my haircut.

"Wonderful. So healthy. I have never seen so much color in your face, Lori. But one thing really surprises me."

"I knew it. My hair. You're shocked that I cut my hair. But it's so much cooler and Danni really likes it," I said and saw a look of annoyance skitter across Danni's face.

"No, not your hair," my grandfather replied. "But I don't think that in the past five years I have seen you in an undershirt without writing on it."

"They were polo shirts, Grandpa," I said, and we all laughed.

I sat in the back seat of the car for the ride back to Balfouria, my head resting on my grandfather's shoulder. I had not realized, until I saw him, how much I needed to see someone I was connected to, family that really belonged to me. As much as I loved the Erons and Avraham Macovi and my friends at Sadot HaEmek, they weren't my family. I listened to my grandfather and Avraham Macovi speak of old friends, taking up the threads of their life and trying to weave a fabric of their memories. When I woke, the lights of Balfouria were in front of us and I was startled. For a brief minute I had thought we were on our way to our Vineyard house, my grandfather and I. For the first time in many months I was homesick, and clinging to my grandfather I longed for the touch of my father's hand, the smooth feel of my mother's lips. Suddenly, urgently I wanted a Baskin-Robbins ice cream—almond chip.

"Oh God," I thought, "where do I belong?"

Then Danni's hand pressed mine, and we went into the house together.

CHAPTER FIFTEEN

"It looks beautiful, doesn't it, Lori?" Rina and I stood in the doorway and looked at our afternoon's work. We had spent hours setting and decorating the seder table and we were proud of it.

The table was set for twenty. In addition to the Eron family, my grandfather, and myself, Gad's family had been invited by Esther and Rina had asked Amy and Ellen, who arrived laden with boxes of Barton's candy sent by their families in America and shrieking their inevitable chorus of "*fantasti*—exciting." In order to seat so many, the table had been extended through the living room, and Esther Eron had produced an enormous damask cloth, worn thin with age, but still of an ivory whiteness.

"It belonged to my father's mother," she said as

though trying to explain the presence of the fine, elegantly embroidered linen. "My father tells me that she had several such cloths and they were used only on holidays."

"That is true," my grandfather said. "She served tea every day at the house in Hamburg. A crystal chandelier hung over the table. I remember the way the prisms spilled light across the cloth. Tiny dancing rainbows."

"Was it a big house?" I asked.

"I don't really remember the house," my grandfather replied. "Only the dancing rainbows. When you grow older, Lori, you remember only the important things."

We all smiled then. I arranged the gladioli that Rina and I had carefully chosen from the greenhouse in the cutglass vases that had once adorned that lost table in a distant German city. I knew that I would always remember that on this seder night, the ivory hearts of the tall coral and yellow flowers had exactly matched the color of the cloth.

We used a china service which Esther reserved for Passover. The pale blue plates were the color of the Mediterranean in high summer and had been worn with age to an almost watery translucence. Behind each setting, ruby-red wine sparkled in clear goblets, and Elijah's silver cup stood at the center of the table. The traditional sedar plate was next to Avraham Macovi's setting, and at Chaim Eron's place there was a plate of *matzoth* covered with a strip of embroidered cloth, also worn thin with age, Rina told me that the *matzoh* cloth had belonged to Chaim's mother, her grandmother.

"It is the only thing he has, the only thing he kept with him. She gave it to him before she was taken away. She embroidered it herself, and he remembers clutching it and watching her as she followed after the other women; to the crematoria, he thinks, but he does not know. He kept the *matzoh* cloth beneath his shirt, like a magic shield. Sometimes, he said, he lay awake at night and traced its stitches with his fingers, remembering his mother's face, her hands, her eyes. He had it with him in the displaced persons camp and during the war for liberation." Rina's voice was heavy with grief for her father's losses.

I thought of Chaim Eron's long silences, the silences he had learned as a child who had only a scrap of embroidered cloth to comfort him against loss and loneliness. I bent closer and saw that Chaim Eron's mother had sewn intricate roses of coral satin, entwined with pale green willow branches and that in thread of matching green she had sewn the word "Shalom." I fingered the faded thread for a moment, thinking of Rina's unknown grandmother whose fingers had worked the word "peace" and who had herself been killed in Hitler's war.

Just before evening, when we had placed the candlesticks on the table, Nimra arrived. She carried with her a table decoration. In a straw basket of her mother's fine weaving, she had created a miniature oasis, using olive branches, the cones of the cypress tree, and a tiny dwarf cactus.

"Nimra, it's beautiful," I said, and as I moved closer I saw that her eyes were red and she had lost weight.

She nodded gratefully, and although we begged her to stay for a while, she hurried off. I watched her vanish into the landscape, her purple dress dragging in the dust.

Esther fingered the basket thoughtfully.

"Before the war, before the anger between Jew and Arab, when we first came here to settle, Nimra's grandmother made us such a basket for each festival. It was her way of thanking us, I think, for the medicines and other help we gave her family. This is the first time, since the 'forty-eight war, that they have brought us such a gift. Perhaps, times are changing," Esther's voice was hopeful, and her fingers traced the pattern of Hulda's weaving.

But Chaim, when he saw the basket, frowned.

"Nimra brought it? That is very strange. Always it was Abdul who brought it and then stayed for a glass of grape juice and the first cactus fruit. You remember, Avraham?"

The old man nodded.

"I remember. But times change. Customs change. Even feelings. Sometimes you must change too, Chaim Eron."

He looked at my grandfather, who turned to me and said softly, "You cannot fight your children's wars. And you cannot always protect your grandchildren."

I moved closer to him and looked across the table at Chaim Eron who absently stroked the needlework on his mother's matzoh cloth. Then Esther came in and lit the candles, softly repeating the words of the holiday benediction: "Blessed art Thou O Lord our God who has sustained us, preserved us, and enabled us to light these holiday candles." "Amen," we repeated, and I saw Chaim Eron's eyes still on the cloth made by a woman who had been neither preserved nor sustained.

The guests began arriving, carrying with them bouquets of flowers, bottles of wine, boxes of chocolates. Chaim Eron, with Danni in a dress uniform on one side, and Udi, easily balanced on hand crutches on the other, welcomed them. I thought of how soft and loving Chaim looked when he was happy. It was only when he felt threatened and unhappy that the tight lines of hatred twisted his features. But then he bent to kiss Rina, who looked so beautiful that night, dressed in a blouse that matched the ruby redness of the wine, her hair caught back in a chain of early spring roses. She moved away from him, her anger and hurt battling her love, and I saw the anger flash across her father's face.

But it was gone when we gathered about the table at last and Avraham Macovi began to read the Haggadah. Gad's small brother Noah asked the four questions, and the answers were sung in a sweet chorus: "Wherefore is this night different from all other nights?" "Because we were slaves unto Pharoah in Egypt. . . ."

At home we had always had a seder, either in my grandfather's house or at a hotel, but all I remembered was a ceaseless mumble until at last the dinner was served. Here there was singing and talk, and when one of the children asked a question, the service would stop while Avraham Macovi offered a careful, thoughtful answer.

"Why did God kill the Egyptian babies? They didn't do anything wrong. It was their parents."

In the child's small, high voice I heard the echo of my own question, and I remembered my last urgent conversation with Liesel. She was not responsible. She was of another generation. It was not her guilt; it was her parents'. The questions went on and on, and there were no answers.

Avraham Macovi struggled to reply, explaining that sometimes a whole nation is held responsible for the sins of a few, that sometimes injustice happened and could not be easily explained. The child looked at him dubiously, and Avraham blushed and continued the reading.

And then finally the meal was served. Rina, Esther, and I scurried from the kitchen to the table, passing out plates and collecting them. Matzoh crumbs created small hills on the cloth and there were streams of spilled wine on the cloth. We ate and talked and laughed, and now and again a song broke through. Again and again the wine glasses were filled, and we drank toasts to freedom and liberty, to peace and brotherhood.

"May God who creates peace in the firmament, create peace for Israel and mankind," Gad sang in his strong controlled bass, and the chant was picked up around the table. The small boy who had asked about the Egyptian babies fell asleep, and we spoke more softly now, so that we would not wake him.

Then at last the dishes were cleared, and it was time to read the second half of the Haggadah. We opened our books again and in the sudden silence we heard the child's even breathing and smiled—at his peace and our sweet sense of community. Danni's hand covered mine and I smiled at him. From their seats at opposite ends of the table, the two old men, our grandfathers, looked at each other. I turned back to Danni and saw how his hair turned the color of copper in the glow of the candlelight. I added my voice to his in the singing of the hymn to Elijah the prophet as the door was opened for the legendary wise man.

"Elijah, the prophet, come swiftly and bring peace in our time," we sang and automatically looked toward the open door.

No prophet stood there, but the night was ablaze with flames, and we sat paralyzed with horror as a volley of explosions ripped through the darkness.

Danni and Chaim dashed upstairs and came down again with their rifles. Udi went to a drawer, dug between papers and handed two small handguns to Gad and his father. Shoulder-ing torches, the men quickly left the room. Esther was already in the kitchen urgently shouting into the telephone, and Rina had gathered the chil-dren about her and taken them down to the base-ment air raid shelter.

We heard the sound of shots, and Avraham Macovi and my grandfather doused the candles and drew the curtains.

"Grandpa, Avraham, go down to the basement with the children," I begged, but the two old men shook their heads.

"We have the luck of the old on our side," Avraham said. "Am I right, old friend?"

"You are right. But you, Lori—you go and help Rina."

I started off but stopped as a ricochet of machine gun fire sounded, followed by an eerie silence. And then a voice shouted wildly, urgently through the night.

"Rina! Rina, are you all right?"

It was Yaakov's voice.

Footsteps thundered outside our door and then it was flung open. Instinctively, I moved beside my grandfather who stood quite still, and to-gether we looked at the men in the doorway. A group of Israeli soldiers stood there, their Uzis poised, their breath coming in harsh gasps. Yaakov Gamliel led them. His uniform was caked with mud and a ribbon of blood ran across his cheek where a bullet had grazed it.

"Lori, thank God, you're all right. Where is Rina?"

"Here," she stood in the doorway, leaning against it for support, as though any moment she might given in to that terrible weakness that I, too, felt. "Oh Yaakov, you're all right? You're really all right?" She slumped then, and he ran and caught her before she slid to the floor.

"Rina." He kissed her cheeks, her eyes, raised her hand to his lips and carried her over to the couch.

She opened her eyes then and saw his face. Her fingers traced its way through the blood on his cheek.

"Nothing. A flesh wound," he said and buried his head in her lap.

The door opened again and Danni and Chaim came in, followed by Gad and other men of Balfouria. They moved slowly, their weapons heavy in their arms, their eyes clouded as though they had seen too much. Outside, in the distance, we heard the moan of a man in pain and then the sharp sudden shriek of a mountain jackal.

"Chaim, what happened?"

Esther moved quickly toward her husband, her eyes searching his face, her hands clutching his. It was not the first time she had seen him come home from battle. She knew the signs to search for, the questions to be asked.

"We were lucky. They planted explosives in the small barn. That was what caused the fire. But an army patrol saw the flames and the leader moved quickly." He turned to Yaakov who had stood when Chaim came in, Rina's hand still in his. "I thank you, Yaakov Gamliel. You are a brave man."

He crossed the room and solemnly shook Yaakov's hand, and then he bent and kissed Rina gently on the cheek.

"Esther, the boy's face must be cared for. Go Yaakov. Go with Esther." He used the voice he reserved for his sons—the quiet caring tone of a man fathering his children. In that voice he welcomed Yaakov into his family, and the dark young soldier quietly followed Esther out of the room.

"The small barn?" I asked in a quivering voice. Danni put his arm around me.

"I'm sorry, Lori. Shalom-Salaam is dead. The barn burned to the ground, but because of Yaakov and his soldiers the fire did not spread."

"What of the terrorists?" Avraham Macovi asked.

"They were led by Ibrahim Nashif. He was killed. The others were captured," Danni replied.

"Then Abdul Nashif has been sheltering them all this time?" The old man could not believe it. He and the Arab were friends. They played *shesh besh* together in the shade of the olive trees. They talked as the quiet shadows of evening fell and together they walked through the fields studying the crops.

"No," Danni said. "According to what the men say, Abdul would not give them shelter. One of the reasons they chose Balfouria was to avenge themselves on Abdul. They saw his friendship with you as betrayal. But of course the Nashif family did not report Ibrahim and his men to the authorities. That was wrong."

"That is because they did not know they were here," Avraham Macovi said firmly.

"But they did, Grandpa," Danni protested.

"They had to."

"No. It is too much to ask—that a man betray his kinsmen. And what will happen? Suppose we say that he knew and should have told us? We will avenge ourselves on Nashif whose family has been good to us. New seeds of hatred will be planted in his children and the cycle will begin again; from one generation to the next and we will have no peace. Somewhere the hatred must stop. And tonight it stops here. There will be no more talk of the guilt of the Nashif family."

He looked around the room and then resumed his seat at the head of the table.

"Come we have not completed the Haggadah. The seder is not over. Bring chairs for the soldiers."

And so we took our seats again. Yaakov sat beside Rina, their hands tightly clasped, as though they would never again let each other go.

It was my grandfather who led in the singing of the final song.

"An only kid," he sang, "that my father bought for two *zuzim*. One kid. An only kid."

I pressed my face against Danni's chest, knowing that it was foolish to weep for Shalom-Salaam when no lives had been lost and no one was seriously wounded. But still I missed my camel, my little camel, my only camel.

I came down to breakfast the next morning and saw Abdul Nashif, wearing his dress suit and a spotless kaffiyah, solemnly shaking hands with Avraham Macovi. He was just leaving and I saw that both their coffee cups were empty. He bowed to me on the way out.

"Do you want to know why he came, Lori?" the old man asked.

I nodded.

"He came to tell me that he had decided to send Nimra to the university. He said that last night had convinced him that somewhere the hatred had to be ended and he wanted to open up new pathways. Those were his words. New pathways for new lives. Strange how things end and how they begin."

"Yes," I said and looked through the window to the charred ruin of the small barn. Just beyond it I saw the flowering almond tree, heavy with bell-shaped white blossoms. A gentle breeze caught up a flurry of black cinders and tossed them through the air so that they mingled with the falling petals. As I watched, Yaakov and Rina came walking hand in hand toward the house, quiet smiles of joy on their faces.

CHAPTER SIXTEEN

The school year was over, and our little group of Balfourians had come through pretty well. Rina had taken honors in her comprehensive exams, and Gad and Rafi, through some miracle, had managed to get their matriculation certificates. I almost fell over when I found out that I had gotten a top grade in physics. That led to a conference with my academic adviser who toted up all my credits and reported that if I stayed on in Israel for another semester, I'd be able to return to Chatham as a graduating senior. I would stay on in Israel until about March and reenter Chatham the following fall for my last year. And I'd have a couple of months free with no school, no obligations—just time enough to be Lori and have a breather before I shifted from one life to another. That sounded good. I didn't exactly want to rush from the fields of Balfouria to the corridors of Lord & Taylor. In the flurry of letters that followed, my folks agreed, the headmaster at Chatham agreed, and I soared on a new kind of high—I was pleasing everyone else and myself at the same time. A Lori Mandell first!

A celebration was in order, and we decided on a trip to Eliat. Danni managed a two-week leave, and while Rina headed for Sadot HaEmek (only this time Chaim Eron, Esther, and Avraham Macovi drove her there, loading the car with gifts for the Gamliel family), Amy and Ellen, Gad and Rafi, Danni and myself headed southward in the pickup truck. It didn't take us long to get set for ten days of sun and sea. We pitched our tents, made camp, and watched Amy and Ellen dance up and down the beach, shouting their usual *fantastis*. Then Danni and I left them to cook supper on Esther's rusting hibachi while we walked barefoot across the rose-gold sand.

In the distance, a sunfish with bright orange sail skimmed across the water. Behind us, on the beach, some American kids with a mandolin and a bass guitar were playing "Turn, Turn, Turn."

"*To everything (Turn turn turn.)*
There is a season, (Turn, turn, turn)
And a time for every purpose under heaven.
A time to be born,
A time to die;
A time to plant,
A time to reap; . . ."

I hummed along softly and Danni sang the words in Hebrew. Barefoot, walking across the fine damp sand, we followed the surf line. Each time I saw a shell or a bit of sea grass I liked, I stooped to pick it up. Soon, I had so many that I held out my peasant skirt, making a basket of it, and dropped them in.

"And what are you going to do with all those shells and stones, Lori?" Danni asked teasingly. "You can't take them all back to America."

A sudden sadness stole over me. I dropped the edges of my skirt, and my sea treasures scattered across the sand. I sank to my knees and tried to find a tiny violet conch shell I had especially liked.

"All right. What's the matter, Lori?" Danni knelt beside me. We were so close to the sea that a wave rushed up and touched our outstretched fingers.

"Nothing," I said stubbornly. Then I saw the hurt and concern in his eyes. "Everything," I added.

"Like what?" He built a tiny tower of translucent pebbles and watched it scatter silently across the sand.

"I don't see how you can be so casual about my going back to America in just a few months. Don't you care that I'll be going thousands and thousands of miles away and you may never see me again? I mean the thing that seems to concern you most is whether or not I'll have to pay overweight on my shells," I said and I was surprised at the bitterness that crackled in my voice.

"Come on, Lori." Danni put his arm around my shoulder, but I didn't respond. "You know that none of this is true. The best news was your decision to stay in Israel another six months. You know I do care about your going away, and there is not a chance in the universe that we won't see each other again."

"Oh, of course. When you finish your degree you're going to come to the States for graduate work. I forgot. After all, it's only four years off. What's four years between friends?" My voice was harsh and strangely familiar. Then I recognized my tone—it was like my mother's when an argument reached fever pitch. Stop it! I told myself sharply.

"It won't be four years," Danni said softly. "First of all we have the next few months together. And then you will come back to Israel, or I will come to America, or we will meet in Europe." He rocked backward on his heels now, his arm no longer across my shoulder. He had found a stick and with it he scratched drawings across the damp, packed sand.

"Great." My voice was toneless. Why was I doing this? I thought furiously. We were on vacation. We were supposed to sing and laugh and swim and sunbathe, and yet here I was deep into what every freshman girl knew should be avoided at all cost—Angry Confrontation and Where Do

We Stand? Lori Mandell, you are an idiot, I told myself. Marcie wouldn't believe this scene.

"Look, Lori," Danni said in that dry, hard voice that reminded me of his father when Chaim Eron was angry. "I don't want you to go back to America. Already I can feel the loneliness of your leaving. Really, I don't want you to go." He took up a thicker stick and added to his sand drawings. A star. A house. A small diamond. A wave rippled up and erased it all. We shifted position so that we sat on a small incline and faced the descending orange sun.

"Then I'll stay forever. I'll go to university here. We'll be together." How light the words were; how simple the solution. I didn't want to leave Danni, and he didn't want me to leave. I would stay. "Dear Mom and Dad—I've decided to stay in Israel permanently. . . ." "Dear Lori—As you know, we have always said, whatever makes you feel happy and fulfilled. . . ."

"No!" Danni's voice came crashing down. "It wouldn't be right. You know it wouldn't be right, Lori."

"But why not? Look at Rina and Yaakov."

"Rina and Yaakov are different. They know exactly who they are, what they want from their lives, and how they feel about each other. Can we say that about ourselves—about each other?"

"Yes," I said defiantly and then I looked into his eyes, so troubled and searching and honest.

"No." My voice was very soft.

"But we do know that we care for each other;

that this has been a wonderful year and that the months we still have together will be good ones—will give us time. But Lori, I don't really know yet what I want to do with my life. When I get out of the army I'll begin university. All I know is that I want to study agriculture. I don't know if I want to teach or do experimental research or if I want to live on a farm or a moshav or maybe a development town. I've never been any place out of Israel. I want to travel—to go through Europe, America, maybe even South America or Australia. I'm not ready to make plans, to settle down, the way Yaakov and Rina are. And you're not either. You know that."

I didn't say anything. The sun had died, and now violet streaks ripped across the sky and turned it a pale yellow. I watched as a family near us prepared to leave.

"Be honest," Danni continued. "Can you say that you know what you want?"

"I want to be with you," I replied, fighting to keep the sob out of my voice.

"That's not enough. You've told me yourself that that's what your mother did. She got married before she knew who she was and what she wanted. It's no good to wake up ten years later and discover that being with someone isn't enough of a life; that you want to be a lawyer or a musicologist or a doctor. Someone has to pay then. You were the one who paid in your family, Lori. Do you want to repeat all that?" He lit a cigarette, and we watched the smoke spiral up toward the violet sky.

"No," I said and I felt a new calm, a calm edged with sadness. Something had ended and something had begun. I shivered, and Danni put the field jacket that he carried around my shoulders.

"What do we have then?" I asked in a small voice.

"We have the next few months. We have the year past. And we have plans and hopes for the future. We'll write. You'll come back to Israel. I know that your grandfather wants to come back."

"Yes, he does."

I remembered how, the night before my grandfather left, he and Avraham Macovi had taken a long walk around Balfouria. I was on the porch strumming my guitar and watching the two old men stop at the new greenhouse, the recreation hall, the empty site that had been selected for the Balfouria school—funds for the school had been lost when the shipment of Balfouria orchids had been delayed. Both old men were smiling when they came back to the porch.

"We will have a school at Balfouria, thanks to your grandfather," Avraham said.

"And we have a Balfouria thanks to Avraham Macovi," my grandfather replied. They were two courtly German gentlemen, transplanted to this Galilean mountainside, exchanging compliments, sharing achievements.

Later my grandfather and I sat on alone, listening to the sounds of the night: the long, low whistles of the herons flying south- from Lebanon; the rustle of the thick leaves of the citron tree, fragrant now with young blossoms; the distant laughter of children, playing beyond their bedtime.

"It is a good feeling," my grandfather said, "to feel that your life has counted."

He and his old friend had made their lives count.

Sitting there on the Eilat beach that night, with Danni's arm so gently about my shoulders, his face so close to my own, I knew that my grandfather was right. Danni and I had to make our lives count; we had to make our own decisions separately and alone before we could make a decision together.

"You'll come to America," I said softly.

"Yes, I'll come to America. And perhaps we can meet in Europe."

"Paris," I said.

"No, Greece."

"London then. I'm hungry."

"I'm starved. And freezing."

"I'll race you back."

We scrambled up, and I saw that the first star, had broken through the darkening sky.

"Star light, star bright, first star I see tonight. . . ."

But I never finished my wish because Danni's lips were against mine, and we stood clinging to each other in joy and fear, wrapped in the new darkness that smelled of sand and sea. And then we dashed back to the campground where a small fire blazed and our friends sang softly, out of respect for the great silence of the desert night.

We spent the rest of that vacation week at Eilat, and when I think of it I remember a rainbow of days—the brilliant blue waters of the Red Sea, the ochre-colored mountains of Edom, the shifting of golden sunlight.

Danni and I went into town and spent an afternoon wandering in a startlingly cool, cavelike shop where we watched young craftspeople fashion the smooth blue-green Eilat stone into lovely pieces of jewelry. I bought my parents two large rings set in silver—matching, of course—and as I paid for them Danni slipped a delicate pendant hung on a silver chain around my neck.

"I have one too," he said and pointed to his own.

"We match," I replied in delight.

"Why should your parents have all the fun?"

We both laughed and touched our twin necklaces, a gesture that we knew we would repeat, alone and together through the months and years to come.

We were startled when we got back, to find a new tent pitched on our campsite, but then we saw Udi's small car parked nearby.

"Something's wrong at home," Danni said worriedly.

"Don't be silly," I replied, but my heart began to beat faster.

Amnon, Udi's tall, smiling roommate who had rescued me that night in Jerusalem, poked his head out of the tent. "Hey, where have you people been?" he said. Udi followed him and we saw from his smile that nothing was wrong at Balfouria and that everything was all right with Udi.

"We drive the length of the country to say goodbye and you're off somewhere building sand castles?" Udi said.

"What do you mean, goodbye?" Danni asked.

"Goodbye, au revoir, shalom, l'hitraot," Udi repeated.

"Arrivederci, auf wiedersehn," I added cheerfully.

"Not to you," Udi said. "You, unfortunately, I'm going to be seeing a lot of. That is, when you return to New York in a couple of months."

I tossed a handful of sand at him. A year ago Udi would not have said those words jokingly—and a year ago they would have made me cry. He was a new Udi. But how had it happened? I thought of Pnina's resolute face, her sure and certain glance. Udi had certainly changed since I introduced him to Pnina, but there was something about it I didn't understand.

"I'm going to America for two years," Udi said. "To study and teach at Columbia. The dissertation is finished—defended and accepted. You see before you Dr. Udi Eron."

"He charges a minimal fee for autographs," Amnon said. Udi pushed him lightly with his hand cane.

"Udi, that's marvelous!" Danni pressed his brother's hand and threw his arms around him, and I kissed him and got kissed back.

We celebrated that night with a meal of Eilat fish, grilled on our hibachi, and ears of newly roasted corn which tasted delicious with the wine which Udi and Amnon had brought down from the Nashif vineyards. Nimra was already at Rehovoth, Udi told us, taking a summer course and working in a lab. Rina would be back at Balfouria soon. Yaakov had received his permanent assignment on the Golan Heights, and she would spend the summer at home before beginning her army service. In two years they would be married.

"I'm coming for the wedding," I said.

"Of course you are," Danni replied and touched his pendant.

Later that night, while Danni helped with the cleanup, Udi and I walked to the ocean's edge. We stood watching the little waves break against the shore and smiled as a group of hippies slouched past us, puffing halfheartedly on sweet-smelling weeds and arguing in a language I did not recognize.

"Danish," Udi said in answer to my unasked question.

"You're not supposed to know what I'm thinking," I said.

"Prina's going to Denmark on holiday this fall," he added, as though reading my next thought. "Alone?" I asked.

"No. With Ezer. I expect they'll be married by then," he replied.

"You don't care?"

"No, Lori. Not now. I really don't. You see, Pnina and I were never lovers although when we first met that was what I wanted. And for a time she made me think that it was possible. Or rather I let myself think it could be possible. It was what started me on the way back—back to myself, to a life that would count for something."

I smiled at the familiar phrase. Udi glanced at me curiously and went on.

"Pnina had a brother. Menachem was his name. He was a marvelous athlete—a Maccabiah and Olympic contender. He took a bullet in his back in the Yom Kippur War, came home in a stretcher, and graduated to a wheel chair. He sat in it for two years, and one night he got some of the kibbutz kids to push him to the top of that hill near Sadot HaEmek. He wanted to watch the sunset by himself he said. When they came back to get him a couple of hours later, they found his chair at the bottom of the hill and his body, broken like a rag doll, next to it. He'd released the brake and rolled down. At the kibbutz everyone said it was an accident. But everyone knew what had happened. When Pnina came to Balfouria and met me, she told me later, it was as though she were seeing Menachem again." His voice grew still, and we both looked upward at the star-streaked night.

"I think I understand," I said. Pnina had teased

and flirted Udi back into feeling. She had provoked him into going to Jerusalem. She had teased him into coming alive again, using the only weapon she had.

"I thought I was doing everything for Pnina. The rehabilitation program, the dissertation. But it took only a few weeks for me to realize that I was doing it for myself and a couple of months more for me to realize that while Pnina was terrific—she was never going to be my girl. I really didn't care. There would be other girls. . . ."

"Like Marcie?" I suggested.

"Maybe," he said. "She's a nice kid. You're a nice kid, too, Lori. I gave you a rough time when you first came. I'm sorry."

"We all gave ourselves and each other a rough time," I replied. "I'm sorry too, Udi." I kissed him on the cheek then, and he passed his fingers across my face and gently stroked away the newly fallen tears.

"Everything will work out, Lori. You'll see."

"Yes. I think it will." I touched the smooth blue green stone of my pendant.

We broke camp and started north two days later so that we would be home in time for Gad and Rafi—to report for their induction into the army. We all posed for a group shot just before we left. In the photograph Gad and Rafi have their arms about Amy and Ellen who seem to be mouthing the word *fantasti* and holding two large conch shells. The sun is in Rafi's eyes, and he is squinting and laughing. Danni and I are holding hands and smiling quietly at each other. And in front of us Udi stands, balanced carefully on his hand canes, his eyes fixed on the family of cranes that chose that minute to soar through the bright summer sky.

CHAPTER SEVENTEEN

The next few months flew by. I was taking a pretty full program at school, and with Rina and Danni both away and Udi exploring Morningside Heights, I was the "younger generation" in the Eron household. Chaim and Esther relied on me for a lot of the small tasks that had once been Rina's and Danni's, and I knew that I'd passed an Eron milestone when I came back from the greenhouse one night and Chaim did not ask me whether I'd remembered to check the thermostat.

It was fun playing "only child." I really had been born into the role. I loved shopping with Esther who always listened gravely to my opinions on colors and fabrics. Now, when she bought a bolt of cloth to use for a dress for Rina, she doubled the purchase and made one for me too. Chaim Eron often asked me to come along when he took a short drive, and I even drove up to the Lebanese border with him a few times to deliver surplus foods to the Magen David Adom station there. A fierce civil war was blazing in Lebanon, between Christian and Moslem Lebanese, with the Palestinians pretty heavily involved. A lot of the Christian Lebanese crossed the border into Israel for refuge or medical services. One afternoon as Chaim Eron and I unloaded our crates of lettuce and cucumbers, we heard the shots, then the shrill cries of small infants. Twin babies had been delivered on the frontier the previous night! I remember thinking how crazy it was for everyone to be excitedly celebrating new lives while the air was filled with the sound of death.

Danni and Rina came in for occasional weekends, and then there were hikes and camping trips and picnics until the weather grew colder and we began to feel the chill of the Galilean winter. It was fun, too, to huddle together in the Eron living room, as the first chilly winds of winter whistled down the mountains; we roasted corns and small potatoes on the hearth fire. It was nice when Rina and Yaakov were with us but even nicer when Danni and I were able to be alone with only my guitar and our books for company. Somehow, knowing that we had only a few months together made those snatched hours of Danni's weekend leaves wonderfully sweet and precious.

I spent a lot of time with Avraham Macovi, also. Once we went together to Rehovoth to visit

Nimra who introduced us to her laboratory partner, a tall, slender Arab boy from Nazareth named Yusuf. Together, they were trying to cultivate a new and hardy strain of winter wheat, and we were not surprised to receive a letter a few weeks later, telling us that they had succeeded and won an agronomy prize for their efforts.

"We are calling it the Macovi strain," Nimra wrote, "in honor of Avraham Macovi who encouraged me to come to Rehovoth."

I thought it was great to have a new grain, made possible by two young Israeli Arabs, named for a Zionist pioneer from Germany.

And it was with Avraham Macovi that I traveled to Jerusalem on the day Anwar Sadat arrived there from Egypt, becoming the first Arab head of state to visit the State of Israel. Avraham Macovi and I stood together among the excited crowds that lined the streets and watched the gleaming black limousines streak toward the Knesset. Our voices joined the thousands of others who screamed out their hopes for peace.

"Shalom, shalom!" we shouted. "Salaam! Shalom! An end to war."

We waved the bright flags of Israel and Egypt. I stood next to a young mother whose small twin sons slept contentedly through the excitement; across their stroller their mother had stretched a banner that read: "Mothers of Israel: United for Peace." I thought of the twin boys, newly born on the Lebanese border, and I knew that their mother would happily display a similar banner. It seemed as though everyone in Jerusalem on that wonderful day, Jew and Arab alike, was united for peace.

Back in Balfouria that night, I fingered my guitar and thought of new stanzas for "Where Have All the Flowers Gone." I sang softly, "Gone to gardens every one," thinking that perhaps we were done at last with flowers withering in graveyards where young men were buried.

It was true that in the weeks and months that followed, it became clear that we weren't going to have instant peace; but the spark of hope was there, and the echo of happy voices shouting again and again "Shalom! Salaam!" remained strong and vibrant.

The harshness of winter faded into the warmth of spring. The hillsides of the Galilee were covered with bright red anemones and the first blossoms of the season appeared on the citrus trees. My heart sank as I turned the pages of the calendar. February. March. At the end of March I would fly home. I was excited about seeing my family again and yet I didn't want even to think about leaving Israel.

"You can't have everything," Danni reminded me gently, and of course I knew that he was right.

During the first week in March I turned in my last research report. Classes for the fall semester had been over by the end of January, but now I was truly through. No more work. No more assignments. And I had two weeks of vacation to spend just as I pleased in Israel. I planned them pretty carefully, rationing my time, hoarding my memories for the months and years before I would return to Israel.

I went down to the Negev by bus, traveled back to Jerusalem, and then spent a few days at Sadot HeEmek with the Gamliel family. By some miracle Danni managed to wangle a few days leave and he joined me there. We would have almost five days together before my flight to New York. I willed myself not to think about leaving Israel but only about the joy of having those brief days together.

There is nothing sweeter than the first balmy days of warmth and real sunlight after a wintry stretch, and when Danni drove into the kibbutz the sun turned his earth-colored hair into the color of beaten gold. We talked about traveling, but suddenly we both realized that what we wanted to do with these last days together was simply to relax and be with each other. No plans. No schedules. We decided only to go into Tel Aviv on Saturday to look at the shops and perhaps to stay late for a movie or a show.

We spent Friday afternoon walking along the seashore near Sadot HaEmek. The water birds were flocking northward again, and Danni, who had recently bought himself a new camera, wanted to photograph the migrating egrets and herons. We passed other photographers along the beach.

"The time for really good pictures is in the

early morning," one of them told us, after borrowing Danni's light meter.

"I'm in the army and on leave," Danni told him. "I don't get up early in the morning unless I have to."

We slept late on shabbat morning and then took little Yaffa Gamliel on a long hike. She was doing a project for school on native wild flowers, and Danni and I were soon competing with each other over wild roses and sand lilies. It was late afternoon when we left Sadot HaEmek, and it was the first of my painful goodbyes.

I shook hands solemnly with Yaakov's father who gave me a set of bookends of his own distinctive carving. I gently kissed little Mrs. Gamliel, but Yaffa wept and wept and clung to my skirt.

"Don't leave, Lori, please don't leave."

"I don't want to, baby," I assured her.

"Then why are you going?" she asked tearfully.

"Because sometimes there are things we must do, even if we don't want to," I replied, and Danni looked hard at me.

Traffic was heavy when we finally reached the Haifa Road on our way to Tel Aviv. Although it was a shabbat, the fine weather had been a tempting invitation to many Israelis, who seldom traveled during the long winter months. Children in the backs of open kibbutz trucks sang happily. Small cars, already quite full, stopped to pick up hitchhiking soldiers. There were lots of buses on the road.

Traffic slowed a bit, which was unusual for the

Haifa Road on a shabbat afternoon. Danni fiddled with the transistor radio that we always carried with us—no one in Israel is ever very far from access to news—but the battery was so weak we couldn't get a station. I looked out the window and saw a couple of police vehicles crawling along the shoulder of the road.

"They must be really out to get speeders," I said lightly. Danni frowned, switched the motor off, and reached onto the back seat for his rifle. Traffic had halted completely. Suddenly I noticed a flock of birds winging their way frantically northward. I had seen birds fly that way once before while I was driving up to Cape Cod with my grandfather—when a three-car collision sent sparrows and starlings fleeing skyward in scurrying clouds of darkness.

"Maybe there was an accident," I said.

Danni sat without moving, his eyes riveted on the road, a finger to his lips. The road, clotted with halted cars, trucks, and buses, was strangely silent. Two kibbutzniks got out of the truck behind us, each holding a rifle and moving slowly, quietly.

A child's scream suddenly pierced the eerie silence, and the air exploded with staccato bursts of gunfire and the muted thunder of grenades.

"Get down, Lori. Under the seat. Quick!" Danni shoved me down and leapt out of the car.

I huddled beneath the seat, trembling violently. My palms were wet with sweat. So much for Lori

Mandell, girl heroine. I don't know how long I crouched there while the sounds of gunfire and explosions went off around me. Later I learned that it was only a matter of minutes. When the shooting stopped I lifted myself slowly up. The road was black with smoke, and looking down I saw bright orange and red flames lick a sky that was oddly blue and peaceful.

The air filled with screams of pain, with the soft sobbing of bewildered children, and the deep terrible moans of men and the weeping of women. Above that I heard the shouted commands of police officers and soldiers.

A small car, only a few yards ahead of us must have careened off the road during the shooting and frantic shouts for help came from it. Ambulances screamed in the distance, and a woman's voice called urgently, "A doctor. A doctor for my baby. Please. Please. Help my baby."

"Oh God," I thought and realized that I was crying.

Then Danni was back, his arms around me, his eyes, too, filled with tears.

In that car on the side of the road, a fourteen-year-old boy was one of the dead. Danni had recognized him. He was a clarinetist who played with a youth orchestra that had toured Danni's army camp.

"The bastards," Danni said, tears streaming down his cheeks. Again we heard the cry of the woman who had pleaded for a doctor. "He's not dead. How can my baby be dead?"

In a short while we had the answer to her question, pieced together from the scraps of information we gathered from other people on the road and the soldiers and policemen who passed us. A gang of terrorists had landed on the seacoast in a rubber dinghy. Armed with rifles and grenades, they had commandeered two taxis and then shot up a passing bus, driving off with some of the passengers. Minutes later they stopped another bus, loaded with children and adults, and forced the driver to head south on the expressway. A lone police car had blocked its progress as snipers shot out the tires of the bus. The passengers began scrambling out the windows and the emergency exits, but not all of them made it. The thunderous explosion I had heard was the bus going up in flames, creating a small inferno on the side of a road bordered with small houses built between field and sea.

"Did any of the terrorists get away?" Danni asked a soldier whose sleeve was stained with blood and whose face was black with smoke and dirt.

"We're not sure," the soldier said. At that moment I understood what the word terrorist meant. The murderers of the teen-aged clarinetist and the child of the woman who now wept inconsolably might still be free. Any moment they might jump from behind a sand dune, with hatred in their hearts and death in their hands. I trembled with terror at the thought of them and the evil they had done and might still do. I understood then the terror that every man, woman, and child of Israel lives with every day of their lives.

We stayed on the road several hours, our headlights beamed on the beach to help the units that patrolled the area in the search for any terrorists who might have escaped. Hundreds of paratroopers poured into the area, the flares of their parachutes dazzling the sands with an eerie fluorescent glow. When at last we were able to leave, we had to drive past the burned-out bus. I turned my head and would not look, but there was no way I could block the stench of charred and burning flesh from reaching my nostrils.

We drove back to Balfouria that night. It was not an evening to be away from family and loved ones. And all the next day we listened to the radio. We heard with relief that there were no terrorists still at large. Wrenched with grief, we watched as mourners gathered for the first of the funerals—that of a five-year-old girl, a passenger on the bus who had been clutching a toothbrush in her hand when she died. Was she, I wondered, the child of the mother whose mournful voice I had heard during those moments of terror? The body of an American woman photographer had been found on the beach. She had been out on that peaceful sabbath morning photographing the migrant egrets. Danni and I had walked the coast, taking the same pictures at the same hour, only the day before. It could have been us, I realized and felt deeply ashamed of the relief that flooded over me because I was alive.

"What will happen now?" I asked Danni.

"We must make sure such a thing does not happen again. The raids from Lebanon must be stopped," he said. Avraham Macovi, usually the voice of moderation, nodded.

"It is the only way," he said sadly.

We all knew that something must happen. We heard Prime Minister Begin's veiled warning to the Lebanese civilians, his open promise that ". . . the arm of terror would be cut off." Esther Eron shivered and moved toward her husband.

On Monday, as we listened to the radio, we heard the beginnings of code call-ups—the Israeli army gathering its reserves together. "Will all those who love Varda send her a gift?"—meaning that all members of a certain unit should report to their headquarters. I saw Danni's neck muscles tense and I knew that his code had been called. He would not be with me when I left Israel. He would be fighting on a mountain pass, perhaps dashing across a newly blossoming hill, or soaring through the sky suspended by his flaring parachute. And I would not know if he was alive or dead, safe or wounded.

I watched him pack his kit bag, stowing in it the packets of chocolate and a chunk of wurst which Esther handed him. She sent her son off to war and danger as tenderly as if she were packing for a picnic lunch.

As I watched her hand him an extra sweater for protection against the cold of the Lebanon mountains, I felt that I could not leave. How could I go now? I would wire my parents. They'd understand. And if they didn't, well, that would be one more thing that stood in the shadows between us.

And then Danni stood beside me, his fingers fondling my hair, his eyes thoughtful, smiling the smile that told me that he knew exactly what I was thinking.

"Lori, you must leave as planned. You must take the plane in two days."

"Danni, how can I?" I felt weak with fear and misery.

"You must. For me. Please, Lori. Promise."

I promised. His lips were light against mine, his hand gentle against me. I waited until he was gone and then let the tears stream down my cheeks as Esther Eron rocked me gently in her arms.

All that afternoon we watched armored vehicles trundle northward toward Lebanon, and when the phone rang we dashed to answer it. One call came from Rina. Yaakov's unit, too, had been deployed northward. Tears trembled in her voice.

"Oh Rina, he'll be all right," I said. They would all be all right I assured myself, but I knew, of course, that that simply could not be.

I stood outside that night and watched the first stars gather in the eastern sky. Somewhere, miles to the north, Danni was watching those very same stars.

"Star light, star bright," I whispered into the wind, and I knew that Danni and I were wishing the same wish, praying the same prayers. Shalom. Salaam. Peace.

Two days later I sat between Avraham and Esther as we drove to the airport at Lydda. The offensive in Lebanon had begun the day before, and we listened to the radio as we drove. There were casualties on both sides, but they were not heavy. Pockets of Palestinian terrorists were being systematically eliminated. There was a thrust northward.

"How can I leave?" I asked again.

"You must," Avraham Macovi replied. "I promised your grandfather that you would, and you yourself promised Danni."

"It will be all right," Esther assured me. "You must go. I will write to you as soon as we have news."

She knew, of course, this strong woman who had been a soldier herself and who had sent her own husband and children off to wars, that it was the uncertainty of not knowing that I could not bear. Would Danni be safe? And Yaakov? Rafi? Gad? Who would live and who would die? The awesome words of the Yom Kippur prayer echoed in my mind.

Avraham Macovi stopped the car to pick up two young soldiers traveling back to their camp. They expected to be sent to Lebanon but they were not frightened. Their faces and their voices were very young. They should have been singing of sunlight and green fields. I turned from them and remained silent for the rest of the way.

It was boarding time when we reached the airport, and there was time only for a swift embrace. "I will wire you if there is news," Esther promised again.

Avraham Macovi placed his hands on my head. "God bless you, Lori," he said. "My friend's grandchild and my own."

I tried to control myself but I wept again as I climbed aboard and was guided to a window seat.

I looked out as we soared skyward. I knew that to the north of the peaceful landscape over which we flew, guns were firing and men were dying, but, like the peaceful, blue bay of Famagusta, which I had marveled at only eighteen short months ago, the vista below us showed no sign of blood and battle. I leaned back and wondered why it was that I was not crying.

"Oh, Danni," I whispered, and then the plane soared upward and all we could see were clouds fringed with the liquid gold of the noonday sun.

Udi was here for dinner tonight and showed me some snapshots that he just received from Rina. The pictures were taken during Passover at Sadot HaEmek, and in one of them I see that my little Yaffa almost reaches Rina's shoulder. How quickly she has grown in less than a year's time. Rina looks marvelous in her uniform, although I am sorry that she cut her hair. Still, I guess we're even, because I've let mine grow.

I shared parts of my most recent letter from Danni with Udi. We were both relieved at Danni's news that he would probably get a medical discharge in the next few months and begin the university in the fall. His shoulder doesn't bother him much, he said, but I'm not sure I believe him. He was in a fierce battle in southern Lebanon, and two Russian bullets fired by a

Palestinian guerilla went deep into his right shoulder. I hope that that means he'll never have to fight again, but of course, Danni being Danni and Israel being Israel, that's something no one can be sure of. We write at least once a week, Danni and I, and we're trying to work something out; perhaps to meet in Europe this summer. But even if Danni and I can't swing Europe this summer I will definitely be back in Israel for Rina and Yaakov's wedding next year. They wouldn't dare get married without me!

I'm finishing my final year at the Chatham School and I've been accepted by the Eastman School of Music in Rochester. I used my notebook on Jewish music as part of my application, and if I say so myself the admission people *were* pretty impressed.

"A very mature effort," the interviewer said to me.

"Meet the new Lori Mandell," I told Marcie when I got back from Rochester. "She's mature."

But Marcie didn't laugh. She just looked at me quietly and said, "You know, they're right. You have changed, Lori."

Maybe she's right. Just the other day I was going through a drawer and found a crumpled "baggie" tucked away in a corner. There were three joints inside, and I guess they'd been there since before I left for Israel. I don't know whether or not pot gets stale, but I didn't bother to find out. I flushed it all down the toilet. I'm so busy with school now and into so many things that I don't even have the time to think about turning on.

Marcie and Udi dated for a while, but now they're just good friends. Marcie's off to Berkeley next year, and Udi goes out with a lot of different girls. The girl he brought here for dinner tonight was a graduate student in classics. She grew up on kibbutz and she's been studying here for about two years. I think it would be funny if Udi married an Israeli he met in New York. Ouch! There I go again, thinking of everything in terms of love and marriage. I haven't changed that much.

I sometimes get together with Amy and Ellen. We talk about poor Rafi who was killed in a battle south of the Litani River. He died two days after his eighteenth birthday.

I spend a fair amount of time these days with my mother and father. During the winter we wore our matching sheepskin coats and hiked through the park, and sometimes, in the evenings, if we all happen to be home together (it happens—rarely, but still it happens), I feel them looking at me and then at each other, and I know that those shared glances speak of a love that will shelter me always.

One snowy night last winter I stood looking out the window, watching the falling flakes and remembering the snow that shrouded Balfouria in a cloak of silence and whiteness. My grandfather came up to me and, as though he read my thoughts, he asked, "It was a good time for you, wasn't it, Lori?"

"The best," I said and kissed his cheek, remembering suddenly that I had never thanked him.

We stood together then, at the window, his hand in mine, and watched the snow drift gently down.

The world of tough and troubled teens in Laurel-Leaf bestsellers by

S.E. HINTON

☐ THE OUTSIDERS
$1.75 (96769-4)

Written when Susie Hinton was 16, THE OUTSIDERS became an immediate best seller, with almost a million copies in print. At once tough and sensitive, the Outsiders, a gang of teenagers from the wrong side of the tracks, try to find their place in a world they never made. "Written by a most perceptive teenager, it attempts to speak for all teenagers who find it so difficult to communicate to adults their doubts, their dreams, and their needs."
—Book Week

☐ RUMBLE FISH
$1.75 (97534-4)

Rusty-James, the number-one tough guy among the junior high kids who hang out and shoot pool at Benny's, relies on his older brother, the Motorcycle Boy, to bail him out. But his blind drive to be like his brother eats at his world until it explodes—and this time the Motorcycle Boy isn't around to pick up the pieces. A "Best Books for Young Adults."—American Library Association

THAT WAS THEN,
☐ THIS IS NOW
$1.75 (98652-4)

Mark and Bryon were like brothers, and both became involved in their slum neighborhood's gang warfare. But when they were 16, Bryon discovered things about Mark that forced him to confront a present so different from his past. "A mature, disciplined novel, which excites a response in the reader. Hard to forget."
—The New York Times

At your local bookstore or use this handy coupon for ordering:

Dell	**DELL BOOKS** **P.O. BOX 1000, PINEBROOK, N.J. 07058**

Please send me the books I have checked above. I am enclosing $ _____ (please add 75¢ per copy to cover postage and handling). Send check or money order—no cash or C.O.D.'s. Please allow up to 8 weeks for shipment.

Mr/Mrs/Miss _____

Address _____

City _____ State/Zip _____

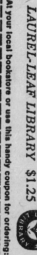